PHILLIP

LANNING'S LEAP BOOK 4

Kathi S. Barton

This is a work of fiction. Names, characters, places, and incidents are products of the author's imagination or are used fictitiously and are not to be construed as real. Any resemblance to actual events, locations, organizations, or persons, living or dead, is entirely coincidental.

World Castle Publishing, LLC
Pensacola, Florida

Copyright © Kathi S. Barton 2015
Hardback ISBN: 9781629893587
Paperback ISBN: 9781629893594
eBook ISBN: 9781629893600
First Edition World Castle Publishing, LLC, November 16, 2015
http://www.worldcastlepublishing.com

Cover: Karen Fuller
Editor: Eric Johnston
Editor: Maxine Bringenberg

CHAPTER 1

Phillip moved through the apartment without seeing anything. He was exhausted and he hurt. Going up the stairs to his bed seemed like too much effort, so he just stripped down to his boxers and sat on the couch. He felt the man in the room before he closed his eyes.

"You should take better care when you are home alone, young Phillip." Phillip didn't even bother answering Nic. "I could have killed you and been gone before you even sat down."

"I'm too tired to fuck around right now, Nic. Go away." The room brightened with light from the fireplace and he glared at the man. "Are you really going to make me pay attention to you? Have you any idea how tired I am right now?"

"I do, and yes. You must pay attention to me. It is very important." Phillip got up and moved to the kitchen, snagging a pair of pants from the laundry basket as he moved by it. He had no idea if the stuff was clean or not, but he didn't want to talk to Nic half-naked. "Trouble is brewing. And I fear that you are going to be hurt most of anyone."

5

"What else is new? I'm so tired right now all I want to do is sleep. I'm beginning to hate this job, if you want to know the truth." He opened his refrigerator and closed it quickly. "I think I forgot to dump stuff before we left this time."

"It is fine now." Nic sat at Phillip's table and a glass of something appeared in front of him. Phillip opened his refrigerator again and wasn't surprised to find it not just fully stocked, but cleaned of all the old stuff as well. He took out the tray of luncheon meats and went to find a loaf of bread. "We have been searching for Grant for you. There is something that you should know. Plenty...but for now, this will be very important to you and your family."

"I'm sure, but right now unless it's a matter of life or death, just give me the highlights." Nic nodded and watched him as he put together four thick sandwiches. It was really too much for him, but he knew that Nic would help him out. After getting a large glass of water, he sat down and handed one of the sandwiches to Nic. "Tell me while I eat."

"Charleston Grant is not dead as we have assumed. Hiding, but not dead. There are others still searching for...Mr. Murphy was not the only one that has been looking. Charlie is human, and as far as I can tell, never had any encounters with non-humans."

"What do you mean, as far as you can tell? Have you seen him?" Nic smiled and shook his head. "What does that mean? You don't smile like that unless you know something very creepy. Not that much of what you do isn't sort of on the creepy side, but right now I'm too tired to figure it out."

"I do not know what you mean about being this creepy person. As for what I know about Charlie, as she tells people to call her, it is very little. Not by that name anyway." Phillip nodded and had taken a large bite of his sandwich when what Nic had said occurred to him. Choking on the bread and meat, he had to take several deep breaths before he was able to dislodge it from his throat before he looked at Nic again.

"She?" Nic nodded and smiled again. "Charleston Grant is a female? You're sure about that?"

"I do know the difference between a female and male, young Phillip." Phillip nodded, not sure he wanted to know anything else about this woman. "She will need to come here, and soon. It is...it will be important to all that she is here and safe."

He wasn't going to ask. Phillip didn't want to know. Not really. She was someone's mate, he just knew it. When Nic got up and poured him more water from the sink, Phillip wanted to ask him for something stronger but didn't. He wanted a clear head.

"Daniel let it be known that she had his book. And those men are after her. Her business was quite successful. She has a great deal of money on hand, all of it cash, and she can hide for as long as she wishes. However, she's not very good at it and someone has let them know where she is. They are closing in on her now and she will be out of options soon. Not just from the men who are hunting her, but other things as well." Phillip asked him what they had to do with it and regretted the question as soon as it left his mouth. "She cannot die. You need her."

"She's my mate then." It wasn't a question, but Nic confirmed it anyway. "I didn't think you'd be able to tell me that. I mean, I guess I just thought you'd let me find out on my own. Fumble around a little until we fall into the bed and then in love."

"It will not work that way with you." Phillip got up to put his dinner on the sink and turned to stare at his friend as he continued. "Charlie will need special care from you. A great deal of it from everyone. She does not see."

"You mean she's blind." Nic shook his head no, then yes. "I don't understand. How can she not see?"

"I'm not sure how to explain it. I've never run into this kind of problem before." Phillip didn't know either, and if Nic didn't, then it was going to be something he wasn't sure he was going to understand. "She is ill. Very much so. Not from the running, but an illness. I have helped her a little, but she will need you to convert her so that she might live. Her mother is with her now."

"You think that will save her? And make her see?" Again, he said he didn't know. "This is not the least bit helpful, you know that, right?"

Nic stood up and stretched. "I did not want you not to have the opportunity to fumble around some. But I must go to her now. She is in danger as we speak. You and Misha, you will need to go and get them. Bring them here as soon as possible."

When he disappeared, Phillip cleaned up his kitchen. He was currently house hunting, having decided that after seeing how much fun his brothers were having in their homes. Living in an apartment wasn't really something that he was enjoying. His neighbors could be heard at all times, and that was driving him nutty. Phillip wondered if he should wait until his mate came to....

"Well, fuck."

Sitting down, he stared off into the living room, which was darkened now that the gas fireplace was off, and thought about what Nic had told him. His mate was the elusive Charleston Grant, and she was sick. He knew nothing more about her other than…well, even that was an unknown to him. How she was ill. His cell phone ringing in the living room had him go to where he'd dropped his pants and answer it on the third ring.

Misha didn't sound all that happy either. "Nic was just here. Motherfucker scared the shit out of me showing up like he did." Phillip told him he'd been there as well. "Did he tell you about this Charleston person and the mom? That they were in trouble? And that we're going to have to help them?"

Phillip wondered if he'd told his brother about her being his mate and decided to wait and see. "He said that Grant would have to come to the compound to be safe. You suppose that he might be wrong?"

He was hoping but knew that Nic was right. "No. He told me that you and I would have to go and get them. That they're in some deep shit. I don't mind telling you that I want something to go normal for a change. Normal would be good."

"I agree." Phillip knew then that Misha didn't know anything but what the rest of them knew. "When does he think we should go?"

"In the morning. He'll be here at nine to pick us up. I guess that Thomas is going to go too, to help with bringing him here. I guess he's sick or something. Did he tell you what from?" Phillip told him that he'd not said. "I guess you should stay here then, for a little while anyway. Just to help keep this guy safe."

Phillip didn't think that once he saw the woman that he'd be able to go anywhere, but said nothing like that to Misha. After a little more conversation about what time he was going to be there, they hung up. Phillip turned on all the lights in his small apartment and looked around.

This place was much like his other brothers' homes. Not the married ones, but the single ones. Andrew prided himself on the fact that he only had a bed in his place, and nothing more than a stool that he ate at the counter with. There was a fridge, but he was pretty sure that he'd never even plugged it in since it had been delivered a few weeks ago. Phillip knew that if he went out on the deck at Andrew's place, he would see that the only thing that was out there was a big box with his grill inside, and nothing else. He'd not even bothered putting that together.

Rider might have had a little more stuff fixed up, as he actually lived in a house and not an apartment. It was being built now and as rooms were finished, Rider was living in them. Phillip thought it was crazy, but then it was Rider.

Rider would have hated living in boxes because it was something that he could control by emptying them, but he'd be no more set up in anything other than a bachelor pad than Phillip or Andrew. There would be nothing on the back of the couch, no throw blanket like those that were forever on the backs of Misha's and the other two married brother's couches. And he'd bet anything that even though Rider had a house, there wouldn't have been any kind of decorations left over from Christmas. He would have put that crap away the day after. Much like Phillip had done.

Phillip decided to go online while he was already awake and make a better effort toward getting him a house. Or a mate a house. He wondered if he should get one on a single level or...Christ, he didn't have any idea, but looked anyway.

Just as the sun was coming up, he'd marked four of them. Two he really liked, one he was so-so about, but the fourth one was the one he really wanted. It wasn't too far from his family's homes, and he thought the acreage was perfect for him and the rest of them should they come over to run. There was even a lovely lake on the property that had a boat house as well as a boat should he want to purchase it. Leaving a note for the realtor, he made his way to the bedroom to shower and change. Wondering what one should wear to meet their mate for the first time, he pulled out a pair of jeans, his usual mode of dress, as well as a Lanning tee-shirt. Going back to his closet, he changed it out for a nice button down and turned on the water in his bathroom.

While the water heated up, he looked in the mirror. He'd been beaten around this time, more than the rest, when he'd gone into the water to catch the body that had been floating down the fast moving water. The cuts and burses on his body would heal as his broken rib had already. He was alive, and thanks to a little extra magic from his brother and his wife, Phillip would live for a very long time. But Phillip was, like he was pretty sure Carter was, sick of the depressing assed job all together.

The accident up the river had dumped several bodies into it, and there had still been three missing when he pulled the older man out. It was better than the twenty-six that had been missing before they'd gotten there. But Misha had told the people they were done in and had to leave. It wasn't like them to leave before all were accounted for and Phillip, like the rest, had been surprised by the move. Until they got on the plane.

"I talked to Linyah and she said it was done. There would be no finding the bodies simply because they weren't there. It was a scam." Rider had asked him what he meant. "Two men are claiming their spouses were on the bridge when it collapsed. They're hoping to get in on the money that is going to be flowing when the attorneys get started on this."

Phillip had been shocked. Not as much as Murph had been, but then she was new to this kind of search and rescue. And being a former cop, she'd wanted to go and find the men and have them brought to justice. Thomas assured her that it was being taken care of, and Phillip was sure that it was.

Phillip was nearly to his brother's house an hour later when he heard from his realtor on the house that he wanted. He could afford it, no problems. But he would not pay the asking price if he didn't have to. The realtor agreed with him, pointing out that rarely did anyone ask what they really wanted for a house.

"Let me do some talking and I'll get back to you sometime today. I have some insider information on the house and it's been on the market for some time. I will tell you that the owners are very motivated to sell, and perhaps we can get a much better price." He told her to do what she could. Pulling in the drive, he assured her that he'd be available if she needed him.

Before he left Misha's with Nic and Thomas, he asked Hannah to look into the address of the house he was interested in. He wanted some first-hand knowledge on the place, and even some reassurances that the place wasn't a total mess. She assured him that she would, and Max said that he would as well. The little guy was going to hang out with them today, as Murph and Carter had some things to look into about her dad's estate. Phillip wasn't looking forward to this.

~~~

Charlie felt the air around her move gently and tilted her head back to feel the sun on her face. It wasn't like her to be idle, but she knew that she was being watched right now and let herself relax. Her mom would never do anything to hurt her. Nor would she let anyone hurt her. But they'd been on the run for a while now, and she just knew when they were being observed now.

"You should know that men...four of them...are coming toward us." Sitting up, she tilted her head. "To your left, love. Just beyond us about twenty feet or so. I have my gun out, so you know."

"Don't shoot them yet, all right?" Her mother would shoot them, too, if they made a false move. "It might be that guy I was telling you about. He's really tall and his hair is fairly long."

"I think it's him. He's with three other men. One of them is big, like strong big. The other two are as well, but younger. Those three are related. They look too much alike not to be."

Charlie knew that the two of them were safe. For now. But in a few days, less more than likely, they'd have to move again. Nic had assured her that they were being cared for and that no one would bother them. She didn't have any idea why she trusted him, but he'd helped her with a few things and she had it in her head and heart that he was one of the good guys. And he'd promised her that he'd watch over her mom when things were settled in a couple of days too. Charlie had had enough of the pain in her head and wanted it to end now.

Charlie knew that she only had weeks to live, more than likely less than that if the way she was feeling was any indication. It had been coming on for a while now and she knew, as did her mom, that it wasn't going to be long. Mom just had no idea how soon it was going to be.

The tumor in her head had gone too long without anyone knowing it was there for much to be done about it. And now it was too late. It had taken over the part of her brain that would eventually shut down all her body, and she'd die. Nic had promised her, after the second time he'd come to see her, that he'd make sure that she did not suffer when the time came. Nor would her mom have to see her in that condition. It was the only reason she was willing to meet with these people today. They were going to take her mom to someplace safe.

"Mrs. Grant? We're here to help your son." The voice was very cultured, and Charlie waited for her mom to correct the speaker. When she didn't, Charlie started to speak when the man did again. "We're here to see Charleston Grant. We've been told that he's in some serious trouble that we can help him with."

"It's a her, Misha." The other voice, the other brother she assumed, sounded pissed. She wasn't sure why, but Charlie thought that she didn't care for the man. "It's Charlie Grant, and she's the younger woman, aren't you?"

"I am." She'd answered him before she could think that she shouldn't. "And you would be Mr. Lanning? The one that is going to take care of my mom?"

"I'm here to see you, yes, and if this is your mom, then she's welcome to come with us too." Charlie stood up and felt the shadow of the man tower over her. She was tall, almost six foot, but he felt bigger than her. "I'm Phillip. This is my brother Misha and my other brother Thomas. And I'm to understand that you know Nic."

Nic touched her shoulder, and she heard a soft growl. Charlie felt the hair on her arm dance at the sound and wondered what the hell that was. Before she could ask, Nic was laughing and letting her go.

"Charlie? What do you mean, he's to take care of me? I do not need taking care of, young lady. I'm very capable of taking care of myself." Charlie felt her eyes, useless now that the tumor was pressing against her optic nerves, fill with tears. She was going to miss her mom so much when she died. "Charlie?"

"They're going to keep you safe from Mr. Murphy and his goons. They can do it better than I can now." Her mother touched her, warm and comforting. "Mom, you know that they're coming. And when they do—"

"He's dead. Daniel Murphy is long gone, but you're right that more than just him are after you both." Charlie hadn't heard that the bastard had died, but was too busy trying to think how to convince her mom she'd be safer with these men to think about it. When the man spoke again, she knew that he was closer to her, and she felt her body wanting to sway to touch him. "I'm going to...we're going to take you back to our house and keep you safe."

"I'm not going anywhere but back to the apartment and hide out." She had more plans, but her mom didn't have to know that. "So if you'll take her now, she'll be fine and safe for me. Nic and I have an—"

"I can no longer keep you safe." She turned to the sound of Nic's voice. "You will need to go with these men now. Both of you. He will...Phillip will need to care for you both now."

The other man—Misha, Charlie thought the man's name was—laughed. It wasn't like he was making fun of her or the situation, but that he'd found something incredibly funny. And for some reason she was pissed about that too.

"I will not be going anywhere without you, young lady. I have spoken to you this...."

The sound, very distant yet sharp, had Charlie turning her head toward it. She knew the sound…a gunfire report, and something that had been hit. "Mom, where are you?"

"Here." Taking her mom's hand after fumbling for a precious second, she backed away from the men. "Where is he, Charlie? Can you hear him?"

Close was all she knew. The sound—a gun being readied to fire again—made her skin crawl up around her ears. Backing up, she hit something solid behind her and cried out. The arms at her elbows had her pausing. The whispered voice at her ear made her shiver.

"Where did you hear it from?" She told Phillip to the north. "All right. I'm going to wrap my arms around your waist and we're going to move. As one. Your mom is with Misha, and Nic and Thomas have gone to see to whatever it is you heard."

"I can't go with you. Nic said he'd help me." The arm at her waist was firm, and she put her hand over it. "Don't let anything happen to her. She is all I have in the world."

"Not anymore." She had no more idea what that meant than she did a great many things lately. But before she could ask him what he meant, she felt movement, fast and very dizzying. Holding tighter to the man that held her, she closed her eyes. It didn't make much difference, but she did feel better for it. When the movement stopped, she held onto the man just a little longer simply because it felt good. He moved his mouth near her ear, and she could have sworn he nibbled on her. Then the heat of his body was gone from hers.

The smells were different. She knew that the dump that they were hiding in, her mom and her, was in horrible shape. The smells alone made her think of old abandoned buildings, and even if her mom had not described it to her, she would have known it wasn't in the best of neighborhoods. But this place did not smell anything like that.

Pine, like a Christmas tree, was strong in the air. She could smell vanilla and sugar too, and wood burning in a fireplace. Charlie reached out her fingers to move and touched the man again, and had no idea why she knew it was him. When he curled his fingers into hers, it felt as right as anything she'd ever done before. She pulled her hand from his, and he didn't fight.

"Where is my mom?" He laughed a little, and Charlie felt embarrassed. She'd been sharp and harsh and that wasn't like her. "Can you please tell me where my mom is? And for that matter, where I am?"

"You're in my brother's home...Misha's house. Your mom is here, too, but in a different part of the house. I think she's with my sister-in-law, Hannah. That would be Misha's wife." Reaching out again, she took his elbow when he offered it to her. "We're in the living room. Right in front of you is a sofa. It's about three inches to your left."

The warmth of the fire had her moving toward it a little, and he told her to be careful, it was huge. As her toes touched the hearth, she knew he was right...the fire blazing from the area was enormous, and she put out her hands to get warm. It seemed that lately she was never warm enough...or for that matter, rested enough.

"Why am I here and not with her?" Phillip said that he wanted to talk to her. "About what? I want to go and see her to make sure that she's all right before I go."

"And where do you think you'll be able to go? You can't see to drive, not that I think your blindness would stop you. I bet given enough time, you'd do just about anything. And since I'm pretty sure that you have no idea where you are, you're not going to be safe out there once you go. How am I doing so far?" She wanted to hit him, and she was pretty sure he knew it. "Also, as I said, I wanted to talk to you. About what you are to me and what sort of things you might know about my kind."

"Your kind? You mean men?" He told her no, he was more than that. "How did I get here without you driving me here? And I want to see my mom."

Charlie felt weak all of a sudden. It was coming on her more and more often of late, and she reached blindly for something to sit on. The man put his arms around her again and she had no choice but to lean heavily on him. Blood — she knew what it was without being told — poured from her nose.

He picked her up suddenly. Charlie might have protested, but she knew she wasn't getting over it this time. That was another thing, it was taking her too long to recover. Letting her body go, having no choice on that either, she felt herself being swallowed up. She heard the man saying her name, shouting it really, but there was little to nothing that she could do about it as darkness took her away.

CHAPTER 2

Phillip watched her sleep. Nic had brought him her medical records about an hour ago, and after reading them three times, he was no closer to understanding what was wrong with her than before. He understood the tumor that was taking over her brain, but very little else. And when she'd fainted in his arms, it was all he could do to calm his poor cat. There was so much information on her condition that he couldn't tell how to help her other than to do what came natural to his kind. When someone opened the door behind him, he watched as his mom came in with Charlie's mom, Dottie.

"She's getting weaker all the time." Phillip nodded and slid the file under his chair. He was sure the woman knew most of what her daughter was dying from, but he didn't want her upset when he talked to her. "Nic and Maribel said that we should talk. I don't suppose you're some fantastic brain surgeon and can fix her, are you?"

"No, ma'am. I'm not." The woman nodded sadly. "I'm not sure what they told you. Or what you know about her condition."

"Condition? I know that in a few short weeks my daughter will be gone from me. That the tumor in her head

19

is eating away at her, and not only will she die, but she will be in so much pain that nothing can take it away." Phillip nodded. "Can you help her?"

"Yes. I think." His mom patted him on the back and left them. "Do you know what a shifter is? What a paranormal is?"

"You mean like they have in those books? Those romance books?" He nodded, then shook his head. "Are you going to tell me that you're a vampire and that you can give her your blood and she'll be healed? I'd about believe anything you'd tell me if that were possible."

"I'm not a vampire." She nodded and looked broken as he continued. "I'm a leopard. A shifter of sorts, as I can only shift into a cat."

She only stared at him for several seconds before looking back at Charlie. He looked at her, too, and wondered not for the first time since sitting down with her what the hell he was going to do. Thinking he needed to talk to her mom about what had to happen, Phillip leaned back in his chair.

"I can convert her into what I am. It will be painful and she might still be blind, but she won't die. At least not from the tumor." She asked him what he meant. "The process is hard on a body and she's already very weak. Weaker than Nic even knew about when he told me about her. She's my mate. Do you know what that is?"

"Again, only what I read in those books. Nic, that other man, he told you who she was to you? Again, assuming that you're not nuts and just a really nice man who saved us today." He told her he might be nuts but not about this. But Phillip had a feeling that she was hiding something. Perhaps her knowledge of what he was or something more. Or both. "She's all I have in the world, Phillip. I've talked to your mom and Hannah. They said that I should talk to you with an open mind. I'm trying, but this is a little more than me thinking you were going to tell me we were going to be safe."

Phillip had another moment of unease. He had no idea from what or why it touched at him, but looking at Dottie and hearing her words didn't set well with him. Liar was all he could think about. She was a liar and it was going to hurt them all. Telling himself that he was overly tired and that he'd been working too hard, he shook his body and smiled at Dottie before continuing.

"You will be. I have a few extra powers in keeping you safe." Boy, was that an understatement. "My family does as well. My brother—Thomas, you met him today—is very powerful, and he said that he'd help me should you allow me to do this."

"Me allow you? Isn't this Charlie's decision?" They both looked at the bed, and he watched her face. He knew when she realized what was going on. "She's not going to wake this time, is she? She's much worse off than she's been telling me."

"Yes, it's progressed that far. And as far as her waking up, I'm afraid that's not going to happen either. I've had someone come here and have a look at her. There is nothing he can do to help her now. The tumor is growing quicker with her weakened state." Dottie started crying, but she didn't tell him he was a liar or rant at him to save her. "She's my mate, as I've said, and she's going to die unless we try and convert her. Thomas said that he'd save her if necessary, but she'll die anyway if he has to step in. Saving her won't prolong her life, only keep what I'm doing to her from killing her. I need you to tell me that it's okay to do this."

"Can you tell me what will happen?" He said that he could and would, but he wanted to tell her something else first. "I'm not sure I can take too much more, to be honest with you, Phillip. It's been a very difficult couple of month's since she fell and we found out what had happened. Then this thing with Murphy hasn't helped either. Too much stress is what is making the tumor work faster."

Nodding, he decided to give her a watered down version of the process. "I'll bite her, as my cat, in several places, which will cause her to be in more pain than anything you've ever felt before. It will be hard on her, so if she lives, we will wait for my saliva to take effect. If it doesn't, she will die. If it works, which Nic has assured me it will, she will be an immortal. Like I am."

"You mean you'll live forever." He nodded at her as that quick unease touched him again. "You do know that this story is getting more and more farfetched as we speak, don't you? I mean, you're a leopard that can live forever, that says he's the mate to my dying daughter. Is there anything else you want to put on me right now?"

"Yes." He got up to pace. There was a great deal more, but he was trying to decide what she needed to know now as opposed to when Charlie was better. "The book that she has, what do you know about it?"

"I've never seen it if that's what you mean. I know that it's important to a lot of people. And Charlie said that it would get us killed. Is that what you meant?" He shook his head. "Then I don't know what else you need to know."

"You should know that I can read your mind." He watched her face and then sat down in front of her. The problem was he could only read parts of her mind. The rest, a great deal of it, was locked away from him. And that bothered him more than her lying to him. "I know that you know exactly what is in the book and what it means to the men who would kill for it. I know that you told Charlie that the police would do you no good, and you know all this because of her father. I know a great deal more, but for now, this is enough to get you to tell me the truth."

"He was a good man, my Curtis, and loved us both very much." Phillip nodded but said nothing to her. "He was a man who kept records for some very powerful men. And while they were bad men, he was a good one, like I said. Up until the day he was killed for skimming money, I'd had no idea he was anything more than just a man who went to work every day as an accountant. The week before he was killed, he told me about something one of his clients was doing and how sickened he was about it. Not that he did any of those bad things. It wasn't until later, after his death, that I knew what he was doing about the money and who he was doing it to. He was an accountant that needed more than they gave him, I guess. And when he was caught, I was just as in the dark as everyone had been. Then they shot him dead one day as he was coming home from work. Of course, they denied it, but who else could it have been but them? Is that who is after her, my Charlie? Are you saying that these men that are coming after my Charlie are like them?"

"Worse," Phillip told Dottie just as someone knocked on the door. Thomas came into the room then and nodded to him. They were running out of time. If they were going to do this, it had to be now. Even he could hear that her heart was slowing. "Mrs. Grant, we have to do it now, or in the next few minutes, it won't matter if they get the book or not."

"Do it." She stood up when he did. "I would like to stay here, if I may. I know that I more than likely will regret this, but I want to be here in the event that she doesn't...in case...you know what I mean."

"Yes. But once I start, there is no turning back. Ever. If you try to stop me, you will be hurt." She nodded and sat down. "I'm going to shift. Don't run. And don't...don't scream. All right?"

"Yes." She stood, then sat down. He asked her if she was ready and she nodded, then shook her head. The terror was there, and the indecision of what she might be doing. He wouldn't have blamed her if she ran. He would have, too, if he could have. When she spoke next, he wasn't the least bit surprised. "I've changed my mind. I'm not staying. I can't. Call me if you can before...if she...I can't watch her suffer."

As soon as she left them, Phillip let his cat take him. When he got up on the bed with Charlie, he looked at Thomas and Linyah, who had come to help. She nodded once at him, and he bit deeply into the soft belly of the woman he knew nothing about. Her scream was enough to make his cat whimper, but he never stopped. Phillip had never been so afraid in his entire life.

~~~

Dottie sat in the little room that she supposed served as a pantry. There were shelves overloaded with canned goods and other things, but she wasn't thinking about that right now. The nice man that was in the kitchen when she'd come in the room had simply opened the door to this room for her and then shut it behind her. The light that was in there with her had gone out long ago. She supposed it was on some kind of motion thing. But since she'd not moved, it had gone out.

Her Charlie was dying, if she wasn't dead already. And for some reason, Dottie thought it was going to end badly for them all. Not that she'd given her the tumor or anything like that, but she was guilt-ridden all the same. A mom should not have to endure something like this. To have a child that you've raised to be hurt the way that her Charlie had been. Things should have gone better for her and Curtis, but they'd frittered it all away like fools.

Charlie had come into their lives one stormy night. She was still a baby, no more than about a month old she'd always guessed. There were things with her...big bags of clothing, formula, as well as toys that the child had never seemed all that interested in. And rules. There had been plenty of those.

She'd been a good child and a great teenager, as well as smart. Her grades were always high, her teachers had loved her, and Charlie could turn ten cents into ten dollars almost in the time it took her to get the money. But she was driven, something that even Curtis, Dottie's husband, had never been.

At the age of sixteen, Charlie had been on her way to making something of herself. Curtis had been working more and more and the money, while good, had been a little sparse around the house because of the fact that they'd been putting it away. Squirreling it, as Curtis liked to call it. So Charlie had started up her own little company to help out the working families around their neighborhood by watching their children while they were at work or just needed a night out. Soon she had several other girls working with her, and they'd shared the profits. It had been a huge success.

Then Curtis had been caught and they'd had to use the plan they had in place to keep him safe. And all the tales about his lifestyle and hers were brought out. They were all true, of course — the money, the spending, and even that the things in their house were all stolen property…gifts from his bosses to keep Curtis happy. Even the cars they owned were stolen, and the VIN numbers all taken off. Charlie had been spared most of that since she'd long since moved out to a bigger city, and no one had associated her with the man named Grant.

It had taken her months to try and prove to them that she'd been as innocent as Charlie about the things that Curtis had done. Longer still for her to get to the stash that she'd put away for herself, money for her to live on in the event that they had to go to extreme measures. Which, as it turned out, had been what had happened to them. That had been a lifesaver, and might still prove to be something that she'd be thankful for should something happen to Charlie. But long before this all happened, Dottie had thought that, after being a mother and catering to the whims of those around her, she needed a break. She needed to live again.

When Charlie had called her a few years ago to ask her to come and live with her and work on this new job she had, Dottie had told her that she was just too busy. There were her clubs and other things that she did, like working at the school to help with some of the children. None of that was true, of course. She just didn't want to be where her daughter could see her all the time. Dottie had enjoyed her time alone, doing what she wanted when she'd wanted. She hadn't even gone to visit her when she'd asked; her life, now that her child was gone, was set the way she liked it.

Then one day, about five years later, out of the blue, she'd seen something on the television about the business called Grant Me Anything, and knew it was her daughter's business. It had told how this company had thrived when others had failed. That the owner, a recluse named Charleston Grant, had been filling orders and getting rave reviews for years now, and not one person had seen him. The woman reporter stood in front of Dottie's daughter's business and speculated on how there must have been hundreds of little workers in the house, because there was a truck coming and going daily to take things out and bring things in. She held up one basket—a gift, she'd said, from one of her coworkers—and said it was the nicest gift she'd ever gotten. Bar none. Dottie wanted to call her daughter then, tell her how she'd changed her mind, when the phone rang. It was her little Charlie, and she'd begged her, once again, to come and help her. This time Dottie said yes.

They'd worked out a way to keep strangers away. To a point that was fine by Dottie. No more hiding from cameras or questions that she didn't want to answer. Or anything else for that matter. Charlie would take the orders over the Internet for whatever a company or person wanted, and Dottie would go online and get whatever was needed to fill the orders. No one saw them. She was pretty sure that no one cared to. Her daughter was a task master, and she wanted to get things done well before they were due to go out.

The trucks came and went, never doing anything more than dropping things off in the front part of the open garage or picking them up in the section marked for them to take. Then she and Charlie would close up the doors and take all the things they had to the big barn in the back. The barn had no windows but plenty of storage space, and when needed, she would store things in the basement. It worked well for her company and the clients that she had, and Dottie supposed that was good for Charlie. Dottie hadn't even missed going out to lunch with her friends, but enjoyed working with Charlie.

Then one day her daughter came from the barn with a book, and nothing had been good since. "It was packed in one of the boxes from that closeout place we got the deals on." Dottie sat with Charlie thinking the worse, knowing that it was going to be worse than that even. "I don't think it was supposed to come with the stuff. I'm pretty sure that whoever this belongs to will come for it, and they won't be happy I have it."

Taking the book from Charlie, she only had to read the first page to know that Charlie was right. This was a book that would get them both killed. Dottie had asked her what she wanted to do with it.

"I don't know. Give it back to them? Surely if I tell them I found it, they'll be all right with that?" Dottie didn't think so and said as much. "I have to do something. I can't worry about this all the time. And you know me, I will. It looks like one of Dad's books. Is it? I mean, I never saw one, but I did watch everything about it on the newscasts."

"I think this is way more than an accountant's notes." Charlie had told her she thought so too. "We should just wait it out. Maybe they won't know we have it. If no one comes for it after...say, a year, then we can toss it. Otherwise, we'll give it to whoever wants it. All right?"

The plan had lasted all of three days, two more than Dottie had been told it would take for someone to come and get it when she made a few calls on her own. There was money to be had on this thing, and she was going to collect. That was when the man with the gun had shown up and demanded that they go with him. How he'd gotten into the house without them knowing was still a mystery to Charlie, and Dottie had let her think that he'd gotten in and not been let in. Nothing about the whole ordeal had gone according to plan.

"You're both coming with me." The man had said he was there to collect. Dottie was nodding as she reached for her purse. "You're not going to need that shit. Just get by the door and bring the fucking book with you."

"Book?" The gun had hit Charlie hard enough to make her cry out, and Dottie nodded again. "I'll get it now. It's in the kitchen. I'll get it, just don't hurt my daughter."

The man laughed, and she made her way to the kitchen. It wasn't in there, of course, but Dottie was going to call for some idea about what was going on. He was supposed to have come to her with her money when she was alone to get the book. When he came in behind her, Dottie had seconds to make a decision. Picking up the sharp knife that she'd been using the night before, she slid it into his throat before she could think what she was doing.

"Mrs. Grant?" Dottie stood up, her heart pounding already from thinking about how easy it had been to kill a man, and she braced herself for the worst. "Mrs. Grant, they're finished."

"Finished?" Jackson nodded at her. "My daughter? Is she all right? Did she die while they did this?"

"I don't believe so. She was doing well when I left them a short while ago. Exhausted, mind you, and still unconscious, but her heart is stronger." She asked him about the tumor. "I don't know, ma'am. I only know that her heart is stronger and that Master Phillip is with his mother."

Dottie was surprised to see that it had been several hours since she'd walked out of the bedroom on the second floor upon leaving them to their work. As she made her way up the stairs again, she tried to think what she was to do now. Her daughter, she had no doubts, was going to be very upset about this. When she entered the bedroom, it was to find that there were others there now, brothers of Phillip she was told, and Maribel introduced her to a man by the name of Danny Hudson, their family doctor. Charlie was on the bed, and she was dressed in a man's shirt instead of the clothing that she'd had on before. Misha was sitting next to the bed, but he didn't move when she came into the room. When she was close enough to see Charlie's face, Dottie started to cry. There was a marked difference in her appearance already.

"Phillip had to go take a shower and get something to wear. He said to tell you he'd be back if you needed him." Dottie nodded and sat down when Misha offered her his chair. "She…it was touchy there for a while, and we didn't think she was going to make it, but she's a good deal stronger than we thought."

"The tumor?" Misha told her that Linyah was going to check, but she wasn't back yet. "I'd like to be here when she takes her to be checked. Do you have a medical facility on site?"

"No. Linyah is…she can tell by just touching her." Dottie just looked at him. "I assure you, she will know better and faster than any x-ray will ever tell you."

Holding Charlie's hand, she looked at her daughter while she spoke. "Those people at the hospital told us that had they had more time, seen it earlier, that they might have been able to take it out. They also told us that it might not have given her the quality of life she'd had until then, but she'd have lived longer if they went digging for it." She huffed. "He said it like it was our fault that no one had detected this tumor before it was as big as a ping-pong ball. By then, he told us it was too late to save any part of her."

"As soon as Linyah comes, we'll know for sure. But I'd not expect her to wake for a while. Danny said that it was hard on her, being as weak as she is." Dottie nodded. "And we don't know about her sight either."

"I don't care about that so long as I have her." Misha told her he'd be back and left her. Dottie held Charlie's hand and spoke to her quietly. "I let him do this to you. I know that you might have said no. In fact, I'm sure you would have. And while I was down there thinking the worst that could happen by agreeing, I realized what you were doing when you told Nic to take me away. You were going to end your life, weren't you?"

It had occurred to her that Charlie was going to try and spare her of her painful death. The doctor had told them, in very detailed information, that it wasn't going to be long, but it would be horrific. Charlie would be in pain, and no amount of drugs was going to touch it. The pressure in her head from the tumor growing larger was going to push her brain into all kinds of overloads before it shut down her bodily functions, including her breathing and heart. It would be, he assured them, the most painful way to die. Dottie was sort of glad that her daughter had been planning to take the easy way out. It would have been really hard on Dottie, and she was sure that in order for her to get to the book, she would have had to stay until the end.

"See what he knew." Dottie brushed her daughter's hair out of her eyes and then ran her fingers down her cheek. "I hope you think I did the right thing, honey. I know that you should have made this decision on your own, but there just wasn't any time. I'm just...I have no idea if anything that young man told me is true either. For all I know, he could have just changed your clothing and then put you here for me to think that you were better."

"I'd never do that." She turned to look at Phillip as he stood by the door. "I would never do that to you or her. She's going to live. I've talked to Nic and he said that the tumor is gone, but that she's been through a great deal and it will take her awhile to recover. But she's not going to die."

"Never." Phillip nodded and sat down in the other chair. She looked at him then and could see that whatever he'd done to Charlie to get her here, to this point, had taken a great deal out of him. "Do you need to rest too? You look like you could use a nap."

"I need to sleep, yes, but not until she's out of the woods. Danny said that she'd need to be watched for the next twenty-four hours. He's not really worried about her heart now, but he doesn't want to take any chances with her health." Dottie asked him what else could go wrong. "I'm not sure, really. She's weak, as I've said, and we did stress her out a great deal by doing this. So we'll just watch and wait."

Dinner was brought up later. Jackson sat with the two of them as they ate in silence. Dottie wasn't hungry really, and from the looks of how much food Phillip left on his plate, he wasn't either. As their nearly full plates were taken away, she sat back in her chair and watched Charlie's chest go up and down until she felt herself drifting off.

The dream started off very slowly. It was her and Charlie, and they were in the barn filling orders. It was a beautiful day, the music was blaring loudly, and the fans that were always on were competing with the noise around them. Looking at Charlie, Dottie smiled to see her so happy.

"Someday you are going to make a man very happy." Charlie snorted at her and told her the man would be in deep shit if she ever married. "No. You'll marry. How else will I have lots of grandchildren?"

Then Charlie was laying on the floor. Dottie didn't see her fall, didn't even witness her being ill. She was just there. And when she walked up to her, kneeling down to help her, a hand, small and childlike, touched her.

"This is a dream." Dottie looked up at the young man. "I'm Max. You know this is a dream, right? That dreams can't hurt you. Nor are what's in them true. This isn't a memory, but a dream. Understand?"

"Is she dead?" He smiled at her and she wanted to touch him for some insane reason. "Who are you? I mean, we don't know each other, yet here you are in my dream."

"I'm Max, like I said. My mom is married to Carter Lanning. You met some of them, I think. There are six Lanning men." He smiled again and moved back from her, and they were in a large forest with brightly colored flowers and birds. "This is better. I can take you somewhere else if you want, but the other dream is all yours."

"I don't understand. You're a real person?" He nodded. "But I don't know you. How are you in my dream?"

"I can do a lot of things. And this is only one of them. But I could feel your pain from the other dream and wanted to help you. I guess now that Uncle Phillip and your daughter have come together, you'll be in this family too." He moved and sat down, and she joined him. "You're hiding something. Something...someone is keeping me from figuring out what it is. You have to tell them. They need to know what you've done."

Then he morphed into her husband, his body big and so healthy, as if she'd seen him just a month ago, that she wanted to run to him. Then he smiled at her, and she could see other things too...the bullet to his chest, as well as the one that had taken out his eye. Her love was truly dead now, and she opened her mouth to shout out the wrongness of it all.

Her body lifted up. She felt the scream just at her lips as she stood up, her daughter laying quietly on the bed, the man who had saved her asleep in the chair. Dottie felt her skin crawl with something horrific, her eyes itching with something as well. Leaving the room, she decided that she was overwrought and needed to get some fresh air. Leaving the house, Dottie decided that her Charlie was in good hands. But she'd be back, and when she did return, she'd get the book. It was going to be her saving grace. Hopefully.

CHAPTER 3

Charlie woke. It wasn't like her alarm went off and she could linger quietly in the bed for a few more moments, but that her body was awake and alive right now. Not moving, she looked around the room and tried to think where she was. The woman across from her made her blink several times just to make sure she was seeing her. Then it hit her like a bat between the eyes. She could *see* her.

"Take it easy and slow down your heart." Charlie nodded but didn't have any idea what she was talking about. "You do. Just think of calming yourself and you will. Slow your mind and your heart will follow. When you're ready, I'll explain what I can."

"Where is my mom?" She said that she had left. "Left? When? I want to see her. Can you tell me where I am?"

"I can. When you're calmer. Being calm is very critical right now." For some reason she believed her. The doctors had told her that it was important that she tried to have less stress in her life or she would tire herself out. "You're doing much better. Much. My name is Maribel Lanning. You met three of my boys the other day. Misha, Thomas, and of course, Phillip."

35

"Can I sit up now?" Maribel helped her to lean back against the headboard of the bed, then sat back down. She was knitting, Charlie noticed then, and looked at the woman's face. "I can see you. I've been...what's happened?"

"Ten days ago you and your mother were brought here. Someone—and we are still trying to piece that one together—found you and fired upon you and the rest of the group. Do you remember that?" Charlie told her that she didn't. Then a man came in with a large bed tray and sat it across her lap. When he left again, Charlie looked at the food before her. "That was Jackson. He's the cook for this household. I had him on a holding pattern for you. Eat, child, and I'll explain."

"I can see. I'd really like for you to tell me now why that is possible." The woman nodded and set her knitting aside. Charlie busied herself with fixing her cup of tea, almost afraid to know the answer now. "I have a tumor in my head. Near the frontal lobe. It was pushing against the optic nerves and causing me to be blind."

"It's gone." Charlie had already figured that out. What she didn't know or understand was how. "What do you know of shifters? Of men and women who can change into something else? Or vampires, for that matter?"

"Know about them? Only what I read. I mean, they must have a book about every kind of animal becoming a person. I even read this entire series about a group of them that formed a clique, and they were everything. Including a dragon." She tried to think what the name of the series was but was coming up blank. "Why do you ask? And what does this have to do with my seeing?"

"You're mated to one of them. My son, Phillip. He is a leopard, as are the rest of us." Charlie nodded. Her mind was buzzing with all kinds of things and she tried to think how to get the woman out of this room, or herself out of here safely, for that matter. "I need to get you on the right track soon because of all the other things that you will encounter now that you can see and are awake."

"Of course. I understand." She ate a bite of her toast and wondered if there was a phone close. She didn't know where she was, but this woman was nuts and she needed to get away from her. "Have you been here long? I mean, are there others like you?"

"Yes. All of us are." Something clawed at her skin, and Charlie nodded while trying to think what to do now. "You're not taking this well, are you?"

"Oh no. I believe you. I was just wondering where the doctor is. Have you seen him today?" The woman huffed at her. "I mean, you more than likely get the run of the place...am I...I lost my mind, didn't I? That's why I'm here and my mom...she brought me here? Or am I dead? I mean, really dead, and this is...whatever that might be called when you die."

"No, darling, you're not dead. Not even close. Phillip brought you here. And we're not in an asylum." The woman got up to pace, and Charlie put her hands under the covers. She was shaking so hard that she could hardly hold her fork. But she felt something move in her head, and she thought about the tumor. Then a man's voice spoke to her.

What is it? Is someone there with you? She looked around the room and wondered how they were doing this to her. *Answer me, please? I'm in the middle of a rescue and I'm afraid I'm not...I've sent Max to you. He's there with my mom. Is that who you're upset with?*

"Someone is talking to me." Maribel smiled and nodded. "How are you doing this? How are you making it sound as if he's in my head?"

"He is in your head, darling. What did he say to you? I'm guessing it was Phillip." The door opened and a young man walked into the room. He didn't come any closer to her, but she pulled the sheet up to her neck, nearly knocking over the tray. "This is Max. I'm assuming that Phillip sent him to check on you?" The boy nodded.

"He said she was terrified." They both stared at her, and Charlie felt her skin crawl again. Looking down at her arm, she could see something moving...fur...and she watched as her fingers seemed to change too. Long claws sprouted from her fingers, and she— "Look at me."

The boy was holding her face in his hands and making her look into his face. She whimpered when he told her to breathe, but she was so terrified that she didn't know what to do. Then the man in her head started screaming at her, and Charlie just closed her eyes and willed herself to faint.

Charlie opened her eyes this time to see a man in the room. He had his head tilted back, the open newspaper in his lap, and a blanket over his feet. He looked...normal, she supposed. She looked around the same room and was glad that at least that was the same...normal.

She supposed that the woman had been too, knitting something in the same chair, but it was the voice and the way Charlie's body had felt that made her lose it that last time. When the paper moved, she looked at the man, and he smiled at her.

"I'm going to try something different this time. I'm Nildale. You don't know me...I'm not what you'd call the best apple in the pot, but I'm not going to upset you, hopefully. Maribel feels just horrible about what happened before. Are you ready, child?" Before she could say anything, he stood up and sat down on the floor near the bed. "There is some urgency in getting you to understand what has happened to you. Your mother, as you have been told, has left the house. We don't know where she is, but we do know that she has made it difficult for you right now."

"I want to see her." He told her that they did as well, but as he'd said she was gone. "I don't know where I am. Or what has happened to me."

"No. I'm sure you don't. And Phillip isn't here to talk to you. He's been on a case for the last several days. He didn't want to leave you just now, but there is...well, we won't go into that right now. How are you?" She told him all right. "Good, good. All right then. You've been changed into a leopard. It was necessary to save your life. Now, I know that you're not believing me, and that's fine too. We'll get to that. There are men after you, as you are also aware. And they've been making some noises, very loud ones, to get you to come to them with the book. I do believe that we should talk about that as well, but for now, we'll just go with you and your mother."

"I don't know what they...it's the book, but I think they want to kill me too. For something that I might or might not know." He nodded and told her that was right. "I don't...why can't I lie to you?"

He laughed. "Because—and this will get you nervous again, I'm afraid—I am a king. My people are the genjar. I know that means nothing to you at the moment, but we are a very powerful and magical race. Since you are related in part to this family, as am I, then you cannot lie to me. Nor can I lie to you. All right?"

"Yes." She thought about the part where he couldn't lie to her. "You say that I'm now a leopard, but we both know that's not possible. They only exist in books."

"You'd be surprised how much they put in those books that is actually real. I do believe that a few of them have been written by actual shifters, but I don't know for certain. But you are as real as I am. If you would put out your hand for me, I'll show you." She didn't want to, and curled her hand closer to her body. "No matter. If you don't believe me, this will be all the more difficult. As I was telling you, you are a leopard. And as such, there will be times when she will get away from you, like happened yesterday when you were upset. You shifted, into your cat."

"That's not possible." He nodded but said nothing more. "I really do want to see my mom. Right now. Please. Right now."

Calm your cat, Charlie. The voice in her head again. *Calm her, love. I need you to listen to everyone for me. Nildale is trying to help you. And he's helping me out while I can't be there. I want to be, but there is too much going on here that they need my help with.*

"There's a voice talking to me. It's Phillip and he said he needs me to listen. And that I must calm my cat." The man in front of her nodded. "I'm overwhelmed right now."

"Of course you are. I can see that. We can all feel it. But you need to be calm. There is a problem that only you can solve. You see, your mother has been less than honest with you. I know that is nothing you want to hear right now, but there you have it." She asked him what he meant. "How much do you remember about your father? Much at all?"

"No. He was killed one day. I don't remember...I wasn't living at home when he was killed, and he was cremated before I was able to come home for the funeral. I...we didn't get along well, Dad and I. He did things that I wasn't...I'm not sure if it was what he did for a living or what, but he was a thief and I knew it. And Mom knew that while I loved him, I didn't much like him. I think that was why she had him cremated before I got home. He was killed on his way home from work or something like that." Nildale nodded. "Has something happened to my mom?"

"Your father isn't dead, child. And the woman that you have called mother for all this time, she isn't your birth mom. Neither of them were your parents. You were being watched, I guess is a good term for it, by them for someone else. Someone that is now after you." Charlie sat up on the bed then and turned away from the man as he continued. "I really hate to tell you like this, but there really is a problem. I need—we all need—for you to remember as much about him as you can...the man posing as your father, I mean. Max...you met him...said that he can't find any memories in your head about him and that someone is blocking him. And from what you just told me, you should have a great many memories of him. But for some reason, they're being blocked, and that's not good for any of us. I think...we all think that he is key to you being chased by this—"

"I'd like to go now." Nildale nodded and stood up. "I want to leave here now and go back to my house. My...my other house. The real one. I have orders to send out, and I need to get them out or I won't have...I want to go home. Right now. I want to leave and go home right now."

She was panicky again. Her heart was pounding in her chest, and it felt as if her mind was closing down. Or moving too fast for her to sort things out. Her skin itched, moved on her body. Refusing to look at it, she was afraid. The man in her head was telling her to be calm, to take deep breaths, but she ignored him. And when

41

something…someone screamed, it took her several seconds to realize it was her.

~~~

Phillip felt the moment that she shifted. And short of screaming at her again, out loud this time, he gripped the arms of the seat he was in and closed his eyes. The touch of the person next to him had him whimper, but Rider told him to just breathe.

"I'm breathing, damn it." He let out a long held breath and sat there with his eyes closed. "Why is she being so stubborn? They're trying to help her and now she's turned into a cat again. I can taste her fear."

"That's why we're headed home." He looked at Rider. He'd not wanted to come with him, but Misha had asked him to not leave Phillip alone. It was probably the best move he'd made. Twice now if it hadn't been for Rider, he would have shifted and killed someone. He might not have been in so much pain then—the throbbing in his leg would hurt more if he didn't shift soon—but he'd been in a hurry to get there. "I don't know why we had to take a flight when we could have simply jetted home on our magic. You suppose it was to calm you before we get there?"

They all had these freaky assed powers now. One— Rider had started calling it jetting—was to move through time and space. Not like they moved, he supposed, but they were just there. But this, he would agree with Rider, was just a ploy to calm him. Because Phillip was anything but calm right now.

"You can't move like that if you're tensed up. That was one of the things that Kendra told us, remember? Remain calm, you must." Phillip looked at Rider when he spoke in that little green guys voice, all Yen like. Phillip decided to change the subject to safer grounds.

"Mom said that she's a beautiful cat. That her fur is golden and black." Rider said nothing, but he knew he was listening to him. "She's going to be really pissed off, don't you think?"

"Yes." He glared at Rider. "Well, if you don't want to know the answer, then don't ask me. You think this is something I want to do? Travel with a tensed up cat that is looking to kill anyone who touches him?"

A woman with a large basket of bagged snacks came by them, and Rider flirted outrageously. Phillip would have, too, under different circumstances, but he had a mate now. One that he knew absolutely nothing about. Phillip looked at his brother's bounty when she finally left them and shook his head. He had five bags of peanuts, six bags of pretzels, as well as an assortment of cookies. And an entire bottle of water with a glass of ice, too.

"What can I say? She likes me." Phillip told him he was going to tell their mom. "No, you won't. You're too stressed to do much more than just go in the house and see to your mate. Who, by the way, is more stressed than you are. Do you suppose we feed off them...I mean feel their stress levels...so much that we are stressed as well? Could cause you a heart attack if things don't mellow out for her soon. You look like a good cross wind would kill you right now."

He had no idea and said so. Then he had a thought. "I should have asked Thomas. Nah, that wouldn't be a good one to ask. He's so relaxed all the time, I sometimes think he's dead. And Misha. He acts like everything will work out and there is no reason to get your panties in a twist about it. Come to think of it, so does Carter. He acts like the entire world could go straight to hell and he'd not give a shit. Maybe it's the sex. That's more than likely it. They are so relaxed because they're getting fucked regularly."

The woman in front of him turned to glare. Phillip realized then that he was talking loudly and that his language was less than stellar. Before he could tell her he was sorry, the pilot told them to buckle up and get ready to land.

The limo was right where it was when they'd left, sitting on the tarmac just waiting for them to return. Phillip knew that it hadn't been sitting there for six days, but it was certainly nice to have it when they got home and were too tired to drive. But this time he wasn't tired, he was scared shitless.

"What are you going to say to her? Hello, I'm Phillip and I'd like to fuck you?" There were times when Phillip wished he was an only child. Like right now. Not answering Rider, he took that as an opening to say more to him. "Oh, I know. Go into the room naked and hard. She'll be really impressed with—"

"I hope that your mate is a real bitch to you. I mean, I hope that she gives you so much grief every single minute of every single day of your life. And now that we're immortal, that could be a lot of grief." Rider said he wasn't worried. "You should be. We've been making notes on things we're going to tell her about you. You should see Misha's list. It's gotta be at least six pages by now."

"You don't scare me." Rider looked way to confident, and Phillip wondered why. "You guys can all have your mates, and I'm going to be the uncle to all your kids that has no children of his own and can pretty much buy then everything. And I will. Every noisy toy, all the nasty stuff that will end up in new carpets, and clothing that will, in general, piss you guys off. It's the way that it should be. One of us will need to be the sane one in the family."

"And you think that you're sane." Rider nodded and smiled at him. "Yeah, right. You're as sane as...well, you're not sane. Not even close. Christ, you're going to be so fucked. I hope she, whoever she is, takes you down a long and bumpy road before you ever get your head wrapped around the fact that you're mated. Yeah, that's my prediction and I'm sticking with it. You are, my dear brother, fucked."

"So are you, little brother." That shut him up. Phillip felt his cat run over his skin, not in a comforting way, but sort of to say, hey, where is our mate? He'd been working on calming him since Charlie woke up, and until today, it had worked. But this morning when she'd talked to Nildale, he'd been really pissy. He felt, and rightly so, that he should have been there when she needed him.

His mom met them at the door. After kissing her on the cheek, he made his way to the bedroom that he'd put Charlie in the first day. He was surprised to find it empty, but just as he was beginning to leave, he heard the water running in the bathroom. Someone was taking a shower. Moving slowly to the door, he tried to tell himself that this was a very bad idea and that he should, if he was smart, run in the other direction. Fast.

Opening the door proved to be the first hurdle, he realized almost immediately. The second was that this bathroom had been remodeled recently and had one of those half showers, the kind that was clear glass up to about chest level, then nothing more. But as she was tall, like him, it was only at just below her breasts...both of them pink from the water and full. His cock stretched in his jeans. Then he heard her sob.

He watched her as she stood crying under the spray of water. It was tearing at him, the way her body was jerking

45

with it. Before he could think that he might have let her know he was there, Phillip moved toward her and reached for a towel at the same time. She turned just as he was handing it out to her.

Neither of them moved. He had no idea why, but he had expected her to scream, or at least ask him what the hell he was doing there. Instead, she turned off the water and reached for the towel, wrapping it around her as she backed to the other wall.

"I'm Phillip Lanning. We met the other day." She nodded. "I see you're up and around now. I guess everything turned out all right for us." He felt stupid the moment the words left his mouth. But she didn't point out to him that he'd had very little on the line when he'd changed her, and only stood there for several seconds before she spoke again.

"I'm a big cat." He nodded and leaned against the wall just to put her more at ease. She didn't move but watched him with daggers shooting out of her eyes. "You did this, they told me. Turned me into this thing. I understand that there was no other way, but I'd like to know what you were thinking when you did it."

"I was thinking of saving your life and nothing much else. And yes, it was the only way to save you, so I asked your mother and she said to do it. To save you." He moved to sit on the counter, the pain in his leg hurting more now. "Your mother gave me permission and—"

"She's apparently not my mother." He told her that he'd not known that at the time. "So this woman, who I've been told is no relation to me, gave you permission to change me and you just did it. To save my life. Maybe I didn't want it saved. Perhaps I was just happy to die."

"Were you?" She didn't answer him. "It's a moot point now. You're my mate and a cat. And we need to talk about some things. Mostly about your mom…Dottie for now, but the rest we can talk about as you need to know."

"You mean as much as you want me to know." He didn't understand what she meant and asked her to explain. "You mean you'll tell me what you think I need to know in whatever sort of time frame you feel I can handle it. I can handle a great deal, and I want to know everything now."

"All right." He shifted off his leg again. "But I have to go sit down on a chair. Or the bed. You can dress if you want, or just wear the towel. I'd like the latter of the two, but I'm in no shape to do much more than drool on you."

He moved out of the room. Phillip was in a great deal of pain now, so much so that he was sort of sick from it. And he was sure that it was going to make him throw up soon if he didn't get off it. Had he been able to shift before getting on the plane he wouldn't hurt like this, but there had been no time. She was in trouble and he'd left as soon as they'd pulled part of the building off him. When she came out of the bathroom still with the towel around her, Phillip finished pulling off his jeans to pull on a pair of softer pants.

"What happened to you?" He pulled his pants up, trying his best not to look at her. But good Christ, she was beautiful. "Are you not speaking to me? Is this another form of punishment?"

It was suddenly too much. The pain, the trip, being worried about her. He turned to her with his shirt in his hand and decided she'd have to do some explaining for a change. Phillip wasn't in the mood to be snapped at or lumped into the "someone hurt Charlie" bundle.

"Who was he?" He started toward her when she didn't answer him. "This other person that has you biting and snapping at me like I'm some monster. Who the hell was he and where can I find his ass? Because right now, I'm not in the mood to be lumped into a group of bastards just because you're all pissy. I'm also not in the mood to be talked to like you are me. Take it down a notch or two or I'm leaving you here to wonder what the fuck is going on."

He saw her face redden, and he moved to the chair. Phillip was really in a great deal of pain now, and he opened up the side of his pants to have a look at his wound.

It should have healed by now. Linyah had told him that the building was full of black magic and that because he'd been hurt by some of the falling debris, he might have a little in his blood. He'd waved her off in favor of coming here, and now he was regretting it.

"Let me look." He told Charlie he had it. "Let me look. I used to be a nurse's aide, and I know a little about wounds. Move your hand."

He did and heard her hiss of breath. "We tried to clean it out when we were waiting on the plane to land, but I don't think we cleared it out so well. I'm going to have to take a shower. Then I'm going to shift and take a long run. I don't suppose we can table this conversation you think I'm keeping from you until then, could we?"

"I'm overwhelmed and stressed out." He said he knew that. Her head was bent over his thigh, and he felt his cock stretch more. He tried to cover himself with a pillow, but she looked up at him before he could get the job done. "You're very...I have to tell you something. I don't know if it's the stress or hormones or the fact that I'm now a cat, but I need you. Badly. Ever since you came into the house, it was like I could feel you there. And I wanted to run you down and fuck you."

"It's because of what we are." He leaned down to just taste her, and she sat up more. He felt her breath on his mouth. "I want to taste all of you. Not just your luscious mouth, but all of you. I can smell you."

"Please." He touched his lips to hers and when she opened her mouth under his, giving him all that he wanted — no, needed — Phillip cupped the back of her head and brought her closer, needing to feel her body on his. But as soon as her hand brushed over his wound, Phillip cried out and fell back on the chair. His vision, everything, just blinked out.

CHAPTER 4

Charlie watched the woman, Linyah, move away from the bed. It had been hard going at first to let her anywhere near the big man lying there so quietly, but then Nildale had come in and held her hand and she felt much better. Charlie could count on one finger how many times in her life she'd wanted to kill another woman as badly as she had this one. And she didn't even know why.

"You're a cat now, dear." Frankly, she was getting sick of hearing that term for everything that was wrong with her lately. Nildale laughed. "I should warn you that I can read your mind. Not all of it, mind you, not the part that is blocked from us, but pretty much what you're thinking right now. While you are very colorful in your description of my daughter, being a cat is the reason why you want to rip her throat out. I wouldn't if I were you. She's very well trained and you will get hurt. While strong, she just can't go against her very nature to try and kill you."

"Can everyone in this family read my mind?" Nildale nodded and smiled again. "You do know that there should be some sort of book on this stuff, right? I'm sure that it's been asked for before, but it would be really helpful to me if I could have something I could gauge things by."

"I do believe that young Max is working on that. However, you will notice soon enough that there are just too many variables with this family. I'm sure that when they started out it was just cats. But now some other beings have been added to the gene pot. Not to mention all the magic. You are, my dear, going to enjoy finding out what you can do now." She didn't think so and looked at him when he laughed again. "Yes, I'm going to enjoy watching you learn, I think."

"You mean fail." He told her there was no pass or fail in this. They both looked at the bed where Phillip still lay. "Well, that wasn't a fail or pass. He was hurt with magic that he didn't understand. So it was a learning experience for him. And all of us. Don't you think?"

"He's all cleaned up. I would suggest he have a nice shower to clean himself up, but I don't think you can hold him up by yourself." Charlie didn't think she could either and told Linyah that. "Perhaps a sponge bath then. His leg is going to be stiff when he wakes up, but once he shifts, he'll be all right. I'd try to keep him quiet until then, but I know better than to try and tell that to a Lanning. I think they were born with an extra stubborn gene."

"Me too." As she made her way to the bed, she thanked Linyah again for her help and the clothing. "I had no idea that he was in that much pain. He just said he needed to have a seat."

"Yeah, that's what I mean." As she moved to the door, Charlie noticed that Nildale was gone now too. Charlie tried not to think about how Linyah had appeared in the room when Phillip had been hurt. Linyah smiled at her as she spoke. "I won't hurt you. Not ever."

"Yeah, you always come into a room with a sword drawn in one hand and a gun in the other when you're not invited, I'm betting. It was all I could do not to run and jump out of the window." She looked at Phillip again. "I don't know what I'm doing here."

"You belong here. As all of us do." Charlie felt the tears again, the ones she'd not shed in the shower this morning. "Can I do anything for you? Hunt someone down and murder them for you? Perhaps find something for you to cut up or beat to shit?"

"Tempting, but I don't think...I don't know what it would be, but I thank you. I don't even know where to begin to think about what I need to do now. This is all so much, and it's coming at me so fast." She looked at the other woman again. "A couple of weeks ago I was making arrangements with a man to take my mother to safety so that I could end my life before...well, before. Now I'm a leopard. I have these strange things going on in my head. My mom and dad aren't my parents. The tumor is not just gone, but I can see again and I'm mated to a man that while I want him, I don't know what I'm doing with him. I'm not sure, but I'm betting I'm missing a great deal more."

"You are. But for now, you should lay down and rest. When he wakes, Phillip will demand a great deal of your attention." Charlie felt her face heat up. "Yeah, and there's that too. Sex with a shifter is very...you're going to have more sex in one day with him than you've had in your entire life. And believe me when I tell you, it will be well worth it. But you should also know that you'll never be loved by anyone like you will by him. You will never want or need anything ever again, and there will never be a time when you will worry that he no longer loves you and has found another. Shifters mate for life. And if that wasn't enough, Lanning men take their loves to heart and keep them there. Forever."

After she left her alone, Charlie sat on the chair closest to the bed. Taking Phillip's hand into hers, she tried not to think about anything but him. And thinking of him didn't make her feel any less overwhelmed.

"I'm not normally so weird or whiney. It's just that you have to admit, it's been very strange for me. Well, you too, I guess, but you knew what was going on long before I did." She felt horrible for blaming anything on him. "I talked to your sister-in-law, Hannah, by the way. And Murph. She's very...well, I was going to say scary, but they all are to some degree. I wish I was more like them. So...so strong. I'm a wuss."

"No you're not." Phillip grinned at her. "You're very beautiful too. I loved your attire from before better. It was much easier to see you than this." She looked down at her borrowed clothing. Linyah had given it to her as she was the only one that was as tall as Charlie was. And since she was also not as chesty as the others, her clothing had simply fit better.

"You mean the towel?" He nodded and moved on the bed, which made him wince in pain. "You're supposed to be resting. I don't know why, but I just assumed you'd be out for a while."

"No. I'm a paranormal, so I heal much faster, even before all the other magic was given to me...to us I guess. And especially since the infection has been taken out. Linyah, right?" She told him yes. "She's a genjar, did you know that? And Max and his mom are Doran. Then there's—"

"No more." He grinned and nodded at her. "Look, we have to talk about all of this. But all I can think about right now is how exhausted I suddenly feel."

"Come here and lay next to me. We'll both feel better. I know that I will." All sorts of thoughts of being in bed with this man made her body warm up. When his nostrils flared, it was all she could do not to lean over him and let him smell all of her. "Christ, I can smell you. You're wet, aren't you?"

"Yes. I've never...what is happening to me?" She wanted to sob, but he moved the sheet off his body and she could only stare at his nakedness. Good Christ, his body was as beautiful as he was handsome. His cock stood up from his body, and she wanted to wrap not just her hand around him but her mouth as well. Swallowing twice, she tore her eyes from his cock and looked into his face. "She said you had to rest."

"I will, when you ride me." He rubbed his hand over his cock and then pulled the sheet down further off his body. She could see all of him now and was very pleased with him. He was thick and hard, precum was just on the tip, and she wanted to taste it. Taste all of him. "Come here and sit on my cock, and you can do all the work while I rest."

Charlie stood up and pulled the borrowed blouse up and over her head. She was bare beneath it. Her breasts were smaller than any of the other women in the house, so she'd had to do without a bra. When she pulled the pants off, taking the panties with them, Phillip sat up on the bed and swung his legs off the side.

"You're supposed to be resting. I'm pretty sure she meant for you to lay there and not get up." He said he was going to rest in a minute and pulled her to him. "I'm going to come as soon as you touch me."

"That's the plan. Fill me with your cum, and I'll feel much better. I know that you will as well." He moved his mouth over her hips, then paused just where her pussy was. "I'm going to really enjoy this."

She thought she might as well. And as soon as he buried his mouth over her, sucking her clit into his mouth, she cried out her release immediately. Backing away from him, thinking him done with her, she was surprised when he not only growled at her but pulled her back for more.

He ate her like he'd never tasted her before. His mouth moved over her pussy, biting and nipping at her flesh, his one hand holding her to him as he devoured her, his other moving between her legs to her pussy. Hungrily he ate her, sliding his fingers in and out of her quicker and quicker until she thought she'd die from the pleasure of it. As soon as she came for what had to be the millionth time, he turned her and sat her on the bed.

When he took her mouth she could taste herself on him. Her juices were spicy, hot, and oh so sexy when he kissed her. As her back touched the mattress, Charlie moved for him, wanting to feel him deep inside of her, his cock pounding her as quickly as his nimble fingers had. The center of the bed seemed so far away because he would not let her do it quickly.

"I want to take my time with you. Explore you." Charlie nodded. "I want you to enjoy this. Enjoy us."

"I am. I've never…this is my first time with really coming. I mean, I've had sex before, but it's never been that…fun." He grinned at her. "Don't make fun of me, Phillip. I'm not stupid."

"I wasn't, love. I was thinking about how much more effort I was going to have to put into this for you. Pleasurable effort so that you never have to think about any sex you'd ever had before."

"More effort from you might just kill me." He lowered his head to hers. When his mouth touched hers again, she moaned when his hand slid up over her breasts and cupped her. Charlie had a feeling that he might kill her anyway.

~~~

Phillip loved the way her skin tasted. The way it puckered under his tongue, how she moaned with each bite. She was perfection, for him and just about any red blooded male. But she was his, now and forever.

Tasting the dewiness of her skin made him move over her to see what other delights he could find. He knew that her left breast had a tiny scar on it that he licked after tasting. There was a small birthmark on her shoulder that he thought looked like a flower. A tattoo that had survived her change made him linger over it, and the design of a small leopard had him smiling. Taking his time with her belly button, her hip bones, and breasts, he laughed when she jerked his head up from her body and glared at him.

"I'm about to die here. Give me some relief or I give it to myself."

Phillip moved his hand down her body to just where her curls were the wettest. Sliding his fingers into her, he watched her face, marveling at the way her eyes darkened as she got closer to her release.

"Come for me, love. I want to see your face when you have your peak. Then I'm going to slowly enter you, take you to such heights that you'll never want to come back." Her begging him made his cock hurt, his spine tingling with his close release too. Moving in and out of her, he moved his body to enter her, his cock, thicker than his fingers, taking their place.

"Please, Phillip. I need to feel you inside of me." Moving deeper, he knew that as soon as he was buried to his root he wasn't going to be able to hold back. So when she cried out, her nails digging deep into his skin hard enough to draw blood, he pounded her, his body not just filling her but claiming her. His leopard begging for his own taste of his mate, he felt his teeth move, his body harden more, and when he came, he emptied not just his body but his heart as well, filling her with his love as he poured all that he was into her.

Biting into her flesh at her shoulder, he felt her mouth over his shoulder too. Tilting his head for her, giving her what she needed, what he needed from her, he felt his cock poise and fill, as if waiting for the moment that she claimed him for herself. And when she bit him, tore deeply into his muscle, Phillip came hard.

Stars danced behind his closed lids. His blood roared so loudly that he heard it in his head. He came twice more, his entire body seeming to need to fill her. He'd lost count of the times that she'd cried out his name, telling him and anyone close that she was coming. His heart felt full, overflowing with his love for her as he dropped over her. Phillip lay there, breathing hard as she lay beneath him.

Moving to his back, taking her with him, all he could think about was how hard he'd come, how many times he'd released. Phillip loved women and had always made sure that they were well satisfied before he took his own pleasure, but this wasn't anything like that. Nothing could have prepared him for how he felt right at that moment.

"I love you." Lifting his hand to run it down her back as she spoke, he was wondering how she even had the strength to move after that when she lifted her head on his chest. "Christ, you killed me. But I wanted to tell you how much…how very much I love you."

"And I do you. I was thinking about...this has never happened to me before. I feel...you drained me. Even my toes are exhausted." Her soft giggle had him pulling her tighter to his body, using any strength he might have gained in the few minutes he'd been laying there. "Now. Leave me alone for about ten minutes and I'll see if I can do that better the next time."

Her laugh was the last thing he heard as he let exhaustion simply pull him down and out. Phillip was never moving from this bed again, he decided, and if he had to, for any reason, he was going to have to be naked, because he wasn't sure that he even had the strength to fabricate anything to wear.

When he woke, the room was bright with light and he was alone in the bed. Moving to sit up, he was surprised at how sore he was. Standing and stretching his big, naked body, he reached for and found Charlie in the kitchen. Whatever she was doing, she was happy for it. Going to the bathroom, he turned on the shower and looked at the man reflecting back at him in the big mirror.

Phillip knew that he was good looking. Women had been at his beck and call since he'd been about ten. The first time he'd winked at a woman she'd actually told him he was much too sexy for a child. Of course, he'd worked on that in the mirror for hours after that. And by the time he was a teenager, Phillip could have any girl he wanted. He'd also realized that sex was more fun than winking had been. Phillip was a womanizer, short and simple. Or at least he had been. Now he was mated and happily so.

Getting in under the hot spray, he realized that they needed their own place. There were things in this bathroom that he'd used before, but none of it was what a woman would use. Thinking of all the things he wanted to do to

Charlie when they got their own home, how they would break every room in, he smiled. Then he reached for the towel when he was finished. All he needed to do about that was call the realtor and tell her he wanted the one that he'd looked at a few days ago.

Entering the kitchen, he was surprised to see it empty of anyone but Charlie and a stranger. As he told her who he was, he noticed that Charlie was staring off into the room as if she didn't know where she was, so he touched her shoulder and she looked up at him. "What's going on?" he asked.

"I've only just been telling her how you two were not meant to meet." Phillip said nothing in response to the woman as he reached for his brother, only to hit a wall. "Your family isn't going to come in here until I say so. And we do need to talk. Things are not going as I have set forth."

"Who are you?" The woman said nothing as she sipped her tea. Phillip touched his hand to Charlie and felt the coldness of it before he reached again for someone to come to his aide. He wasn't surprised that Nic answered him.

I am unable to enter the house without the owner's permission. He asked him what the hell that meant. *The woman that you have in your sights is a fate. Not the three that you know, but another, stronger one that I cannot fight without permission. Permission of the owner of the house.*

Phillip knew he was trying to tell him something, but he had no idea what it was. How the hell was Misha supposed to give him permission to come help him if he had no idea how to —? Then it occurred to him.

Will you find my brother Misha and tell him that I might be in trouble and that I need for you to come to my aide? He said that he would. *Also, I'd very much appreciate it when you come that you bring in all the family. I'm out of my element here.*

Very good, young Phillip. You are much smarter than she thinks you are. Do not let her take your mate. That scared the shit out of him, and Phillip felt his cat move along his skin. *You would do well not to piss her off either. I will help you with that.*

Help me with what? He didn't get an answer, so he asked again. *You'll help me with what, Nic?*

When Nic and his father were suddenly in the room, Phillip grabbed Charlie up out of the chair and shoved her behind him. Misha walked into the kitchen seconds later, and he was obviously pissed off. Phillip's cat wanted out, needed to protect them, but one look from Nildale and both he and his cat calmed.

"Sonya. And to what do we owe this displeasure?" Nildale winked at him as he turned to continue talking to who Phillip assumed was Sonya. "You do realize that this is my family now? And that you are no longer allowed to tangle into their lives? What we agreed on was severed long ago when you tried to take my wife into your lair."

"He wasn't supposed to meet her." No one moved, but they stared at the woman. "You know that the order of things is very important, and I told you when he did not meet her all those years ago that things were going to go as I had planned. Now everything is messed up. I do not like to have my plans toyed with."

"Planned?" They all turned to Phillip when he spoke. "What do you mean, I was supposed to meet her years ago? And what does that have to do with the now?"

"There is an order to things. When you were not where I told you to be, then things were askew. And as I have said, I do not like to have my plans messed with." Phillip looked at Nildale, who was staring at Sonya as well as she continued. "You knew this. I told you that I was finished with this lineage, and you should have listened to me. They were not to meet at all."

"I did nothing to bring them together. Perhaps you have made a mistake and they were determined to meet anyway." The blast of energy took his breath away, and he felt Charlie move to stand beside him. Before he could say anything to her, warn her about...well, about whatever might happen, she looked at Nic and Nildale.

"Why don't we figure out what she means before one of us—and I'm mostly talking about me—shifts into my cat again and hurts her?" The energy level in the room soared up again, but no one said anything. "Misha, is there a place we can talk? Someplace that we can bring the hostility down?"

Misha was laughing when he suggested they go out to the pool and get in it. Cooling off, he told them, would work wonders. Since it was about thirty degrees outside, Phillip thought his joke in poor form but didn't comment. Christ, this was just insane. But Sonya started talking again.

"There is an order. Young Phillip was supposed to meet his mate first. Charleston was to be his mate then, not now." Misha asked why it mattered. "Because I said so."

No one said anything, but then Charlie started to laugh. Then Phillip did. Sonya sounded like a spoiled child. All she needed to do was stomp her foot and the image would have been perfect. Because she said so? What kind of answer was that?

When Sonya lifted her hand up, Nildale stood in front of her. Her hand lowered, but she looked no less pissed off about something. He moved when she nodded once at him.

Phillip had a feeling that they'd all been saved a great deal of pain.

"You know that I do not care for things to be put out of order. I told you that I had a plan for your daughter, and this is not it." Nildale said nothing, but Phillip could tell that he was angry. "I should just make them all no longer have their mates. What would you do then?"

"You'll do nothing of the sort." Misha moved closer to the woman. His cat, bigger than the rest of them, shivered along his skin. "You come near my wife and unborn child and I will kill you. Not easily, either."

"A child? You are to...Nildale?" He nodded and smiled. "This is not funny. I am not to be thwarted in this and you know it. I will only take back this arrangement, but I want you to know that—"

"You think that only Misha would hurt you for touching his mate? Well I have news for you. If you so much as look like you're planning to take my Charlie, I will make you suffer in ways that you cannot imagine."

"Things have an order. When you were to meet her.... Look." She waved her hand and images of them came up. Their mates and how they had met. It was dizzying to see things moving so quickly, but he could see it all. Even when he was supposed to have met Charlie, though most of it was too blurry to make out well. "This is the way things were to go. First you were to meet Charleston, and as such she would never have gotten ill. The book that you are so desperate to figure out would never have happened. Things would have moved smoothly. Then Misha was to meet his mate. She would have been...it was going to be closer than what he came upon, her death I mean, but he would have been happy with her. No children were to be born of any of you. Then Thomas would have met his mate. Linyah would have taken him to the other realm, and they would have been very happy together as well. Carter would have…he wasn't to survive his depression. But the others, your other brothers, would have been happy too. But as I have said, there are to be no children."

As she spoke, images of them continued to blur in front of them until she said their name. But the image of Carter hanging by a rope in the barn took his breath away. Looking at the woman who was telling them that he shouldn't have been alive, all Phillip could think of was that Murph really had saved his life.

"That's enough." Phillip wrapped his arm around Charlie's waist as she spoke to Sonya. "I have no idea what you think this is going to accomplish, but as far as I can tell, you fucked up and now you're all pissy about it. I'm here. Deal with it."

"You cannot talk to me this way. If it had not been for me, you'd be dead by now, along with your parents. They, too, messed up my plans." When Sonya took a step back, Phillip could see that she realized that she shouldn't have said that. "Your guardians will pay for this. Both of them will pay dearly for this. No one defies me."

With that, Sonya disappeared. Misha started cursing almost as soon as Phillip realized that the woman was gone. Linyah and Thomas appeared in the kitchen, along with Sina and several guards. Phillip held onto Charlie as they all started talking at once. It wasn't until Hannah came into the room, put her fingers in her mouth, and let out a shrill whistle that everyone quieted.

"We'll do this calmly and without shouting." To say everyone was surprised at Hannah would have been a gross understatement. But she did move them to the living room where they all sat and waited on some sort of explanation. If there was one.

CHAPTER 5

"Are you saying that you made some sort of deal with that woman in order to get me a mate?" Misha was glad that he wasn't on the receiving end of this anger from Linyah. Gladder still that he hadn't had anything to do with it. She was really pissed off. But Nildale was her father, and as much as he liked the older man, he knew that he'd messed up royally by not telling her what he'd done long ago.

"No. As I have said to you several times now, all I did was ask her to tell me if you had a male in your future. She is the one that said she could arrange it. And if you must know the truth, I didn't think she'd done it. Not after all that time. I figured she'd had a hard time finding one and given up." Nildale flushed brightly. "What I meant was, I didn't think you'd settle for one even if she did find you a male. You can be somewhat stubborn, in the event that no one has pointed that out to you."

"That isn't any better, Father." Misha had to fight against laughing. He knew that if he did it, he'd be hurting. Even Phillip, who had been quiet since Sonya left, was smiling broadly. Linyah was pissed off, and by the look of her, she wasn't backing off anytime too soon. "So she said she'd arrange for me to have a male, and you just simply forgot about it until now. How convenient for you. But that does not negate the fact that she is threatening Charlie. What does she mean that she's going to make her guardians suffer? Her parents? The ones that gave birth to her, or the one that she was raised by? And why have we not found either of them?"

"I don't know." Everyone looked at Misha as Nildale spoke. "What have you found out, young man? Anything on any of them? I know I gave you little to go with, but I can't believe that this is so hard to figure out. What are you using to work on it? Magic?"

"Magic, and even Linyah and Nic are stumped. Neither of them can find any memories of a life before Dottie...and so you know, as far as we can find, Charlie's father is dead. At least the one that was in her life. If he's not dead, then I have no idea where he is." He was confused, so he reached into his pocket and pulled out his notepad. It had been as much a part of him as breathing since they'd opened Lanning Search and Rescue, and using it for everything had paid off more for them lately. "According to what we've been able to unearth about Dorothy and Curtis Grant, they were model parents and good citizens. Up until his untimely death about twelve years ago, everyone thought that Curtis was a broker. I guess in a way he was. But he was an accountant for the syndicate more than anything. And for a big name such as Welshouse. Then after his death, Dottie moved away and no one heard from her again until Nic did."

"How did he die?" Misha glanced at Charlie when she asked and looked back at his notes. "I was told that he'd been killed by being in the wrong place at the wrong time. Driving home after work or something like that. I never really…to be honest, there are some holes in my memory now. I don't know if it's that woman or something else."

"It's more than likely her. And I think she's keeping us from looking into your head for information that is vital. This Welshouse guy is not one to fuck with. As for the way your father died, that's not true so far as we know from Max." Misha looked at his notes again before telling her what he knew. "He was, according to the paper, in an accident, but there are some things wrong with that too. The car that he was driving didn't have any blood in or around it. And his body was never taken to the hospital but directly to the funeral home. Then it was cremated about five hours after he was killed. Or whatever happened to him."

He wished that Max was there to fill in the blanks that he knew they were going to ask him about. Max had gone to classes an hour ago and had yet to return. He was in his last year of college and all of them were excited for him. Max, at twelve years old, was going to be a hell of a surgeon someday, and Misha was looking forward to telling everyone that he was his uncle. Not that he didn't already.

"Max said that according to Dottie's memories of her husband he is very much alive. And so you know, they are actually married, and had been a few years before you came to them. But that, too, is something that we don't know how it happened." He closed his little book. "Her mind is blocked to him as well. Now that we've met Sonya, perhaps he can get in with the help of the others."

"This is just stupid. I mean, I don't even know why there is such a big deal about any of this. She's lied to me my whole life. Why do I care now that she's gone?" Misha looked at Phillip when Charlie spoke, and he looked confused too. "What is it?"

"No one told you?" Both Phillip and Charlie shook their heads. "Dottie is after the book. And the reason you'd been targeted about it is because she's sold you out to the highest bidder, who just happens to be the man that Curtis worked for. Welshouse knows about the book and that his name is in it. Other people, other names in the book, they want it too, before he gets it. Because the holder of that book can control everything."

"How? It's just amounts of money that people owed this Murphy guy. And he's dead. What does anyone care about it now?" Misha stood up and handed her an excerpt from the book. This page was in the back, and it was numbered in a way that had taken them nearly a whole day to figure out. "I don't know what I'm looking at."

"It's what they did to owe Murphy money. Murders. Gambling debts. There are even a few men mentioned in that book that should know better than to get caught at any of this crap, much less doing it in the first place. Senators and lawyers. There are even quite a few doctors there that have been less than above board." As she looked it over, he watched Phillip's face too. He knew that he understood the importance of the book and the names that were in it. "The names in that book will be beholden to whomever holds the book because of the simple reason that they'll be able to hold it over their heads for the rest of their lives."

"You mean whoever holds this book can blackmail them?" Misha told her it was more than that. "What else is there other than the greed for money?"

"Power." Misha nodded at Phillip when he spoke. "Not only will the owner of this book have these people in his pocket, but he'll be able to get them to do things that are well beyond what they did in the first place to get them here. He'd be able to control not just their bank accounts, but anything in their lives. He'll have it all."

Charlie sat there for several minutes, not speaking. He knew that her mind was working. He could read hers as well. He didn't, but the look on her face as she worked through this was scary. And when she got it, not just the importance of the book but also how much it was worth, she leaned back on the couch and stared at him.

"She's sold me out." Misha nodded. "And now that she's gone...she can tell them about you guys and this house. That's why it's been so important for you to know what you think I might know about her."

"Yes. And this thing with Sonya, I'm afraid that doesn't help either. I'm not sure what she can do, if anything, but it's sort of adding to the urgency of what is going on." When Charlie got up to pace, Misha looked at Phillip as he continued. "When you brought them here, did she say anything to you about what she might know? Dottie had to know that this might come out. That she was going to be caught."

"I doubt it. My...Dottie always seemed to think of herself above such things as rules." Charlie continued pacing as she told them more about her "mother." "I'm pretty sure that my father...Curtis had money stashed away for them. I'm not sure, but...it's one of the reasons that I moved out of the house when I did. I was trying my best to make a name for myself by working odd jobs until the money started coming in, and I had a feeling that when the shit hit the fan that I'd be left holding the bag. Then after I was told he was dead, I thought from the way my mom was struggling that perhaps I'd been wrong about it. But I wasn't, was I? They had money."

"And a great deal of it." Nildale moved into the room as if he'd only been in the hall. But Misha knew that he'd been away and had only just arrived. He was, Misha would bet, trying to ease Charlie into their magic. "I just found out from Kendra that someone has found one of his many stashes. I don't know money in your world, but I'd say that if he was skimming, then he had his hands in very deep. There is just over ten million in one place that we've found. The rest, I'm told, will be easier to find now."

When Charlie asked why now, Nildale looked at Phillip. He was frowning so hard that Misha worried for him. But their mom came into the room just then and asked to speak to him. Moving into the hall, all Misha could think about was he hoped that this was a mission. He needed to distance himself so that he could think. But as soon as he entered the hall, he knew that wasn't what it was.

"May I help you?"

The four men standing there had a look about them that screamed armed and dangerous. Whether or not they were legally armed had yet to be established. When his mom moved back away from them he felt a little better, then Rider and the rest of his brothers came in from different directions of the house. He knew then that his mom had gathered her sons to take care of each other, and he was going to kiss her as soon as this was finished.

"We're here to speak with Charleston Grant. Right fucking now."

Nothing more was said, and the man looked like he expected Misha to rush right out and bring her to them. When he cocked a brow at him, Misha laughed.

"You might think I have a clue what the fuck you want, but you'd be dead wrong. And I'm not exaggerating when I tell you, you'd be *dead* wrong." The man asked him if he was threatening him. "Oh no, you have that wrong. I don't threaten. What I'm telling you is that if you continue to stand there and fuck with me, then you will be dead. I'm not in the mood right now to try to be nice. Not that you have been either, but this is my home and what I do is law here."

"Mr. Lanning, perhaps we got off on the wrong foot." Misha nodded but didn't take his eyes off the first man as the second one tried to clear things up. They were both humans, and if they thought they were going to come into his house and treat him like this, then they were going to be dead humans very soon. "We'd very much like it if you were to have Charleston Grant come here so that we can ask her some questions. It's very important to our case. Mark here, he's not had his morning coffee and he can be cranky when that happens." As a joke, if that was what it was, it fell flat. It was nearly four in the afternoon, not the morning any longer.

"And what case is that?" The man reached into his jacket, but he never got whatever was there out before Rider had him on the floor with his hands behind his head. The man couldn't have moved unless Rider let him, and he was pretty sure that the fucktard knew it too. Misha leaned down to talk to him when he noticed that the other men had been equally subdued by Andrew and the others. "You might rethink your way of doing things while here. My family is everything to me, and when someone comes to *my* house and threatens *my* family, I get a little testy."

"Rider, let him go please." No one moved and wouldn't until he said it was all right. Turning to look at Sina, he waited for her to continue and when she did, he could see the anger all over her face. "Let the man go so that I can talk to him. Kendra is most displeased with the turn of events here. These men were sent by someone other than her. And she's coming."

"The queen is coming? Here?" Sina had a ghost of a smile when she nodded at the first man, but the smirking man looked pleased. Even as the first man turned to him, Misha had a feeling that he'd been the one that had interrupted his family meeting. "You said that this was just a pick up. For her. That the queen would be pleased with us."

"I never said she knew, only that she'd be pleased. You assumed that all on your own." Smirker looked at Misha. "You're going to pay for this. She's not going to be happy with you."

"And who would that be?" Kendra looked so regal right at that moment that when the second man dropped to his knees, Misha did the same. But Smirker stood right where he was. Christ, she was one pissed off queen. "I asked you a question and I expect an answer."

"Sonya...Lady Sonya sent us to get the young woman known as Charleston." The man looked too pleased with himself. "She said that you had your head up your ass about this, and that she'd have to take care of it for you. You really should learn to listen to those that are there to advise you."

"Oh really?" The man nodded and smiled. "And just what was she going to do with Charleston once she had her at the castle? I'm assuming that, since you thought I'd be pleased, you were bringing her to me."

Smirker only shrugged. "She was going to allow me to have her first. Then I was to kill her for you. It is a brilliant plan. If this man would only turn her over to me. You should know that he's been very uncooperative with me. I think you should simply end him so I can do my job."

Kendra looked at Misha and then at Phillip. "She also told me that I'd be greatly rewarded."

"You will be. Just not as you were told." With a snap of her fingers, all four men disappeared. When Charlie came out of the living room with his mom, Misha started to tell them what was going on, but Kendra spoke first.

"May I?" Misha wasn't sure what was going on, but as soon as Phillip disappeared along with Charlie, he thought perhaps he'd been had. Then Kendra spoke in his mind. *Bearing witness, my friend. They will bear witness for me and when this is finished, I will return them to you. Sonya is going to pay.*

Misha told the others what Kendra had said and made his way into the living room again. Things were out of his hands for now, and he, for one, could use a good laugh. Telling the others what the little prick had said, they all laughed for a good ten minutes. Misha hoped that it wouldn't be the last for a while. He was getting tired of all the stress they'd been under lately. That included their jobs too.

~~~

Dottie sat in the bus station for over an hour waiting for Curtis to come for her. He wasn't a man that was ever on time, so the wait only made her angry but didn't worry her. One of these days he'd be on time, then that would be the time that she'd worry. Something would surely be wrong if he was where he was supposed to be when he was told. And heaven forbid he should be early for something.

Dottie looked up when she heard something and there he was. She saw him about two minutes before he saw her.

He had been such a handsome man when she'd met him over forty years ago, but she thought this new and improved Curtis was even better. He was thinner, thanks in part to not having her to cook for him, and now that he was taking better care of himself, he was bigger too. Like stronger bigger. But it was his face that was the hardest to get used to. They had paid to have his entire being altered to keep him safe, and she was still trying to get used to it.

"Hello, my love." He kissed her soundly on the mouth then pulled her from the seat. "I would have been here sooner, but I got messed up on the time."

"Sure you did. And I don't suppose that the fact that you smell like beer and cigars has a thing to do with it." Curtis flushed, but only smiled at her. "You're supposed to be keeping a low profile, Curtis. What would I do if you were caught again?"

"No one has a clue who I am. I've told you this before. Even my own mom would have trouble knowing me." She pointed out that she was dead and had been for some time. "She'd still not know me. Anyway, I'm here now and we can get this thing rocking. Did you collect the money like I told you?"

Frowning, she looked at him. Surely he'd messed that up as well. "You said you'd get the money." Her heart started to race just a little when he shook his head. "You did. Tell me you got it, and then we'll go and hide from them all."

"I didn't get it. And I checked. Just to make sure that I had it right. You got it." Dottie shook her head and sat down again. "Dottie, the first stash, it's empty. You got the money, didn't you? I won't be mad if you got it. We'll just laugh about it and go on, like we planned on doing. Okay?"

"No. I never...I never touched it. It was our promise that we'd collect it together. Remember? If the first stash, the one with our identifications in it as well as banking information, is gone, then something happened to it. And that pretty much means that the other monies are gone too. We wrote in there so either one of us could go and get it should something happen." He sat down as well, and she thought he looked like he'd aged several years in those few minutes. "Who did you tell? You had to tell someone, Curtis. Who did you tell?"

"No one." He looked sick, and she knew just how he felt. "Did you? Well, that was a stupid question. Of course you didn't. You lived like a pauper for all those years and didn't touch it. I'm sure you'd not...someone stole our money, Dottie. Someone took all of our hard earned money. That just isn't right."

She supposed they'd stolen it in the first place, so it wasn't really theirs either. But now it was gone. All of it. She was sure that whoever had found the first stash of money had gone on to get the rest, and neither of them had any idea where it all was anymore. There had been so much of it when they'd been working to get it gathered up for their rainy day. They had scattered it around so much that it had taken her over a month to remember them all and write them down. Then the week before Curtis was to be killed, they'd made a pact to gather it in fifteen years. Just the two of them. But this thing with Charlie had come up with those people and she'd had to contact Curtis sooner. That or they were going to ruin it all. And it seemed that they had anyway.

"We have to think." She had all kinds of thoughts now and wasn't sure that much more was going to fit in her head. Dottie wished now that she'd taken some of Charlie's stash and been done with them both, but she'd loved her husband and wanted to be with him when the shit had hit the fan. "What are we going to do, Curtis? We don't have the kind of money to pay for the things that I've set up for us. The house alone is going to be more than we can do each month, even if we could get a job at our age. I was expecting that money to be there and now that it's not, I have no idea what we're going to do." Millions of dollars. Millions upon millions of dollars that they'd worked for was now gone. In the hands of someone else.

"You got us a house?" He sounded so pleased with her that she wanted to hug him. "What kind? Will I be able to have my own office? And bathroom. You know how I feel about sharing a bathroom."

She did know but loved him anyway for it. But they'd not be able to move into the house, not without the money. And buying the furniture that she'd wanted wasn't going to happen either. She'd been looking forward to living in style for so long now that it was a hard blow to know that they weren't going to be able to even eat well, much less live that way too.

"There was this man, a boy really, who told me that he could read my mind. I thought Sonya told us that no one could do that. That whatever we wanted to be kept private would be that." He said that he didn't know but would talk to her. "And how do we do that? She's the one that comes to us. We don't know how to find her."

"I think I might have a plan." She didn't point out that his plans were not all that well thought out, and worse when it came to executing them. He was good with numbers, and that was about all he was good for when it came to criminal activity. "We just have to go and get that kid. She will come to us once we have her. Don't you think?"

"You mean Charlie." He nodded and grinned. "I'm sorry to tell you this, love, but I'm pretty sure that we're fucked there as well. For one thing, she's not a kid anymore. In addition, Charlie is with the people that read my mind. And if they found out about the stash, there's a good chance they know about you as well. And even if that's not true, I'm sure that she's not going to come anywhere near me even if I begged her to."

They left the bus station and made their way to his car. It was beat to shit and looked like it wouldn't go two miles, much less start. But when the engine roared to life, Dottie had to smile. He'd provided for them in this at least.

When he told her that he'd gotten them a hotel, she was excited. To be waited on and have her bed made was something else she'd missed, living the way they had. But when he pulled up in front of a drab hotel that looked like it had been old in the seventies, she sat there staring at it. Nothing, it seemed, was going to be what she'd expected.

"It's not that bad. And we get a free breakfast in the mornings. Plus, when it's done, I get the leftovers. Been keeping me fed for a few days now." She nodded but continued to stare at the hotel. "Come on, honey, we'll get this figured out. You'll see."

As she got out of the car with him, all she could think about was how hard she'd worked to get the money. Curtis had done all the actual skimming, of course, but she'd been the one that had put it away. For a rainy day she'd always told him. And when Sonya had told them that watching over Charlie would give them even more, she'd jumped at the chance.

Sonya had told them that Charlie would be important to Dottie's plans. When Sonya had shown them what she could do, she'd also hinted that the girl would be able to do those things as well. It wasn't until she and Curtis had fallen in love with the girl that they were told that she wasn't anything more than they were. Just a human that could mess up Dottie's plans for the future. They'd never figured out what those plans might have been, nor what problems she might have caused to mess them up. Her love for the child had soured after that. She'd not hated her...she could never do that, but there were times when she thought of what was really going on with her. There had to be something more than just some mislaid plans.

"Do you suppose we might be able to thwart her plans?" Dottie asked him who. "You know, that magical woman, Sonya. She said that we'd be rewarded for watching over the kid. Well, nothing much has come our way. I almost got caught. You had to live like you didn't have a thing, and I had to pretend to be dead. I know that she said that we'd be healthy and at the time, it was good, but now I'm thinking we might be able to get more out of her. Like some cold hard cash."

Dottie had just been diagnosed with cancer the year before they got Charlie, and it had gotten to the point where it was the end of her days. Curtis had been so ill with his diabetes that he was going to have to have a pump as well as his left leg taken off because of it. She'd preyed on them. They knew that, but since both of them had enjoyed great health as well as having Charlie in their lives, it was okay. But not now. Things were nothing like she'd been promised. Not a single thing.

"I don't know how to contact her." He nodded. They'd never had a means to contact her. "But I might know of someone that can. There was this man at the house. He said that Charlie was his...his mate. Maybe if I tell him what's going on, not all but some of it, he can help us get to her."

"Might be worth a try. I have to do something in the meantime, though. I'm...you know how I love my numbers." She did and smiled at him. "I've already gone through about fifty of those puzzle books. But I need more."

"I know. I'll contact him tomorrow. By phone. I don't want them reading any more stuff in my head. Even if it is true, those are my memories and things." He told her that he agreed. "So, what do we do now?"

When he wiggled his brows at her, she had to sigh. Most women would think that meant he wanted to make love, that it was a come on. Not with Curtis. It was a game. He wanted her to give him large numbers to add, subtract, and multiply. She never knew if he was right or not, but it was what he loved to do. So she started giving him five digit numbers to add up. Sadly, that was the highlight of their evening.

CHAPTER 6

Charlie tried not to let her mind drift too much. The two men in front of her were arguing about what was said by the other. The man who seemed to have all the answers, though Charlie doubted that he even believed most of it, was going on about how they were sent to take her and that there was nothing that Kendra, the queen, could do about it. Apparently, he also believed that raping her was fine, because they'd been given permission. Charlie was pretty sure that raping might have been preferable to whatever else they had planned for her.

"And Sonya, did she tell you why you were to take Charlie?" The confident man, Toby, frowned at Phillip as if he had no idea why he was even concerned about the answer. Then it occurred to her that he didn't know her as Charlie about the same time that Phillip must have realized it. "Charleston. Did she say why you were to take Charleston?"

"Oh, yes. Because she wanted her." As if that was enough for him to do her bidding? "We're running out of time here. I should warn you that she told us not to be late or she'd make us hurt. Let me tell you that while I enjoy the pain that she inflicts on me when we're fucking, I'm pretty sure that this will be meaner and not so enjoyable. I'll have to tell her that you're the one that delayed us. And she'll not be happy with you either."

His name was Toby, Kendra had told them. And the other man, the one that was currently lying on the floor in a fetal position, was Ben. Ben had had a change of heart about all of this and had been begging to be killed quickly. Kendra had told him to shut up, and he'd been curled up with his thumb in his mouth since. The other two men had long since been taken away by the guards. But Toby was the real brains...or lack of brains of the operation.

"I'm sure she'll understand when I explain it to her. Where was it that you were to meet her? I'm assuming it was on this plane? This area of my world?" Toby nodded at Kendra when she asked and smiled. It was then that Charlie noticed that his teeth were all gold. He was dressed in rags, less than that really, and his teeth were all capped in gold. "Well?"

"Her home. I've been there several times. So many...we're lovers, you see. And once she and I have taken care of the girl for you, you'll be able to bless our union so we can be one." Kendra asked him why her approval was needed. "Because you are the queen, for now anyway. I surely wish that you would finally release us to wed. It has been too long in the waiting for me. This time you'll do as you've promised."

"You mean Sonya told you that the queen was holding your love hostage, and that if you did this to me, you could marry?" When Toby nodded at her, Charlie looked at Kendra. "This can't be true, is it?"

"No, it's not. This moron has been lied to. For a long time, I would guess." Kendra looked at Toby, and Charlie almost felt sorry for him. When she spoke next to him,

Charlie could see the dawning as it came upon his face. "You don't need my permission to marry unless you are royalty. And neither you nor Sonya are, in any way shape or form, royalty. Sonya is only a sorcerer. Someone that has been...she's not welcome in the castle any longer, and so you know, you won't be either if you survive this. But what I don't understand is, if she doesn't think I'm fit to be queen, why she would seek to have my approval on anything? Especially on something as important as a wedding. Unless she never had plans to marry you. Could that be it?"

"Survive? And of course she wishes to marry me. It's all we have talked about for decades. She wouldn't do this to me." Kendra nodded at Toby but said nothing to his queries. "I have done nothing but work for you. You can't do this to me. I won't allow it."

"*You* won't allow it?" He nodded and crossed his arms over his chest, and Kendra looked at Charlie before turning back to Toby. The man really was a moron. "You cannot allow or disallow anything, you idiot. I'm the queen. And I'm in charge."

"You don't rule me." No one said anything, so Toby continued. "I might work for you. And help out my Sonya, but you don't rule us. You're nothing but a lazy conniving woman who thinks you are superior to the rest of us. No one is better or stronger than Sonya. And she will prove it to you when she takes the Lannings down. You with them."

Kendra glanced at Charlie and Phillip, then looked back at the man. Guards came in then, lining against the walls two deep, their swords drawn and their armor in full regal fashion. Linyah came up to stand behind her sister, Kendra. They were ready for a war. Phillip pulled Charlie to him. If the shit hit the fan, Charlie decided that she wanted to be close to someone that was stronger than her.

Glad for the comfort of his arms around her, she watched the man. He had to know that the guard had entered the room. They were surrounding them all. But he seemed as unaffected by it as the fact that Kendra was his queen and that she was very unhappy. When he smirked, Charlie wondered if the man was stupider than they had first thought him to be.

"Just so I have this straight. You don't think I rule you, yet you need my blessing to marry Sonya. She's at some time told you that in order to marry, you need my approval. Is that right?" He said it was. "And you think to please me by killing this woman and bringing down the Lanning family, which I'm sure you realize is my family—and my entire royal court as well—just to please a queen that you do not recognize nor do you think rules you. You do realize that makes no sense whatsoever, don't you? I mean, really?"

"You aren't the ruler, but some lazy sack of a thing that makes us all cater to your every whim. Sonya has told me of the things that you demand of the ones that think you are the greatest thing that has come to us. You are nothing to us. But I do need for you to bless our union. Before we have to kill you." Phillip asked him what kinds of things Kendra demanded of her people. "She has someone bathe her. Did you know that? She cannot even remove her own clothing without several servants to do it. And when she is in the wrong, which is very often I'm told, she has the person killed. Like she did her physician a few months ago."

"You mean the one that tried to kill my sister-in-law? That doctor?" Linyah said. Toby nodded and said it was the way things were done when Kendra was displeased with things. "You say that she's not your queen, yet as she pointed out, you want to please her. What sort of pleasure would she get from having my mate killed? Not to mention, having my entire family brought down? Tell me, Toby...what has Sonya told you about the Lanning family?"

"She said that you do nothing all day but sponge off the backs of our labor. That our kind, including the queen, sees to your needs when you do nothing in return for us. My Sonya would be a better queen. Her magic is powerful and good. While you...all of you are nothing but power hungry grubs that make me sick."

Phillip moved toward Toby, and before anyone could stop him he put his hands to his head. The scream of pain was all the warning they got before the guard moved as one to protect the queen and Charlie.

Charlie had no idea what Phillip had done to the man. With his hand on his head, his fingers at his eyes and ears, she thought for sure that he was going to tear his face off. When he lifted his hand from him, there was no blood nor bruising, but that didn't mean that Toby wasn't in pain from his touch. Charlie watched as Phillip leaned down to the moronic man and spoke quietly to him.

"Do you see that? Can you see what I do when I work? And that is only one day in the lives of my brothers and myself. We work hard, as does Kendra, every day to keep people like you safe from yourselves." Toby whimpered and nodded. "Does that look like a family that does nothing all day? Do you see one of your kind there that is not related to me? Do you see me having myself fanned with great foliage while I dig in the mire and mud for bodies? Bodies that your kind has put there? No, you don't. Do you want to know why? Because it's easier for you to lay blame than to find out facts for yourself."

"No."

Toby fell to his knees. Blood poured from his nose and mouth, then his mind, Charlie could see, wasn't doing well with the information. Kendra moved toward her and gave her a small push toward Phillip. As Phillip continued to talk to the injured man, Charlie touched her fingers to his arm and he looked at her.

"Enough, Phillip. He's had enough. You can't teach him anything. His heart and mind are frozen to the truth." He stared at her as if he had no idea what she was talking about. "Phillip, let Toby go. You're hurting him."

As soon as he stood up, Toby fell to the floor. He, too, was now curled up, his thumb in his mouth, as he sobbed that he knew that they had lied to him. Even as they stood there, the guard picked both men up and took them away. Kendra was escorted to a set of chairs not far from them just as her father came into the room. Charlie looked up at Phillip.

"What did you do to him? I'm assuming that you showed him something that you have done." He said that he had. "I didn't know you could do that. Didn't know...I don't know a great many things, I think."

"I can help you." They both turned to Nildale when he spoke. "You'll need it, I think. To have the knowledge that comes with being what you are. To have it all would keep you safe for me...for us all. I would—and this is because I have come to love you like family—I would very much like for you to be prepared for Sonya when she comes. I have a feeling that she's going to hurt a great many of us before we catch her."

"I saw it." They all turned to Phillip. "I saw what she has planned. It was…it's in his head. He…she's going to bring war to your lands. There are others, more races that would like to have all that you are, and when they come — because they will — they're going to destroy all that you are. Including beheading the royal family for their crimes against their people. Sonya needs to be stopped now or she'll bring them here. And they think it will end badly for not just your people but all mankind as well."

"Has she contacted them as yet?" Phillip told Kendra that Toby thought that she had. "I doubt it then, but just to be sure, I'd very much like to figure out what she thinks she will gain from this. And I've no doubt that she thinks something is coming her way. And it will, just not what she's expecting it to be. The nerve of that woman."

"She hid Charlie from me." Kendra asked him how. "Sonya had Toby and five other men kill her parents, then kidnap Charlie so that we'd never meet. She's right, we were to meet first, Charlie and me. And her thinking was that if we didn't meet and mate, then the rest of the fated relationships of my family would never have happened either. She thought that once the first cog in the wheel was removed that nothing else would go forward. That was her plan. To weaken you as a queen because of the strife between you and Linyah."

"Good heavens. She's nuts."

Charlie laughed. She had no idea if it was what Nildale said, the way he said it, or simply the stress of it all. But she laughed out loud. When they joined her, she felt better for it and leaned on Phillip. Nothing had ever made her feel as good as being with him did.

~~~

Phillip hated to leave the house, but as soon as he returned from the castle, they were called out. Kendra told him that she'd send someone to watch over the families and that they'd be safe while they were gone. He felt better about it, but was still hard pressed to leave Charlie right now.

"There are five people missing this time. Two adults and three teenagers. The car they were riding in was discovered about ten miles from their home. Riddled with bullets we've been told, but no blood. The police are thinking that it was shot up after they were out of it. What they don't know is if it was because the family was already gone when they got there, or if they were leaving a message after taking them." Misha handed him a thick file as he continued. "The husband is a lawyer. And the police are trying to rule out that this was a crime against him. But the house, their home, had been ransacked pretty messily, and they can't find his computer. So far they've not turned up anything electrical, such as phones, computers, or any other device like that."

Murph picked up the conversation when Misha sat down. "We've had the phones pinged, to see if we can get a signal off them, and we've gotten nothing. Either they've been destroyed or they're somewhere away from the family. I'm thinking destroyed. The laptop that the police are most interested in is a company one. The firm that he works for said that Mr. Rainer had access to the entire company, as he worked at home most days. I've had someone go in and set up a fire wall, but since the family has been missing for an undetermined amount of time, it's hard to say if we've shut up the barn after the horses have been let out." She handed him a sheet of paper. "That's the phone numbers that were received or called out to just before the phone suddenly shut down. Can you look them up for me when we hit the ground?"

"Sure, but I can tell you right now that three of these numbers are a pizza place." She asked Phillip how he knew. "The number is the same for this company nationwide. See? I've called this same number and it all goes to a central location, and their pizza orders are sent to the store closest to you. Doesn't always work out well, but most of the time they get it right."

"So someone ordered pizzas. Can you find out how much and where they were taken?" Phillip said he would and called the number. In five minutes he had the manager on the phone for the local office in his town, and he was able to breach some security to get him what he needed. It helped that the guy was a shifter, and they'd been running together since they'd been kids. He told them what he knew as he worked on the other four numbers.

"So they ordered five pizzas four days before they left, then ten the next day. Sounds like...I don't know. Can three teenagers eat that much pizza, you think?" Rider assured Murph that they could, no problem. "So we can assume that they got the food for themselves. The credit card company is giving me a hard time about getting the last known usage of their cards. But the company that he works for is sending what they have on his company card now. They don't think we'll find anything on it but a few company meals. I guess Mr. Rainer is a straight up kind of guy."

Andrew said he'd make a few calls on the credit cards and banks. As he moved to the back of the plane to have some quiet, Phillip continued trying to figure out the rest of the calls. Nothing seemed to be out of the ordinary until he tried calling the last one to verify.

"Seventy-six and Weston." The line went dead almost as soon as it was connected to the person. Phillip started to call the number back, thinking he'd gotten the wrong number, when it rang again. Before he could say anything, he could hear voices in the background and hushed everyone around him to listen. The plane got silent just as someone spoke again.

"I asked you where it was. Now you'll either tell me this time or I will break your other leg." A small whimpering sound made him think that the person was in pain. The sound of something hard hitting what Phillip knew was a hand made the person cry out. "Now, we're going to do this again. Where is the money? All of it. I swear to Christ, I've had enough of you and your bullshit."

"I don't know what you're talking about." There was a scream this time and the phone was dropped. Phillip wondered if that was the end of what they were listening to when someone spoke in a low urgent whisper.

"Please hurry. Seventy-six and Weston." Then the line went dead.

No one moved. Phillip stared at the phone for a long time before Murph took it from him. He had no idea what she was going to do until she put it on the floor and crushed it. Misha asked her what the hell she was doing.

"It's a trap." Rider asked her how she knew. "Okay, several things. But first of all, how did they know where they were being held? Usually, that's not something the kidnappers tell their victims. Then, and this is the kicker, why assume that the person on the other end of the line is going to know what the fuck you're talking about when you just give an address? If a regular Joe Blow answered that call, they'd just think it's a prank, then hang up. On both calls. She didn't say come and get me, I've been kidnapped and they're killing my dad. Nope, just the street address."

"Okay, but what else? And why did you kill the phone?" Phillip knew and told Misha. "Okay, so they can track us with it. I understand that. So you're thinking this has to do with us and not just the family."

"I do. And the other things are not lining up either. Like the car...why shoot it up? That just screams foul play at you. Why not leave it in a parking lot with the doors and windows locked? Now you've just told the world you have the family."

Phillip liked where this was going. Not that it was a trap but that they were working it out before anyone got hurt. When Andrew came from the other room, he looked confused.

"The cards have been maxed out. I asked my buddy at the office about it, and he said that it's normal for the card's balance to be low, but about six weeks before, they'd maxed it out. Nearly eleven grand on the one card alone. He said he'd bet that all of them were like that...the man and woman have two each with the company. I called the other two companies they have cards with. It's the same, they're all maxed completely out. Nearly a hundred thousand in purchases." Phillip asked him some of the places the purchases were made. "Yeah, that's weird too. A suit was ordered but returned. Then there was the couch and love seat set that was bought and paid for, then returned."

"Thirty days." Everyone looked at Phillip. "After thirty days the credit card company will give you the option of getting cash or taking a credit on your card. I've done that before. My bill came due before I decided to return the dresser and they asked me that. Since I'd paid off my card, I didn't want a hanging balance. I think they were padding their cash with buying things, waiting the right amount of time, then taking the cash in return."

"Why?" That was, as far as Phillip knew, the ten million dollar question. Misha continued when no one answered him. "Okay. So they have about a hundred grand, give or take however much they already had. Or for that matter how long they've been doing this. Something spooked them into running. Or they have a plan to get us there. I'm more inclined to think it was just them running, but I have no idea."

When the plane landed about forty minutes later, they were no closer to figuring it out than they had been before. But one thing they did know was they weren't going to go to the address without back up. As soon as they were at the home base, Phillip could see that Thomas had been busy. There were about fifty men there ready to help them out, all of them from the castle. At the last minute, however, Charlie contacted him.

"Don't take the king or Nic in. I know that telling Linyah not to go is like telling her to go ahead full force. She's sort of stubborn like that, but if this had to do with Sonya, this is the perfect way for her to get to some of them." He was so stunned by the idea that he didn't speak for several seconds. "Or that could just be a crappy thought. I'm sorry I bothered—"

"No, it's brilliant. I think you might be right." He moved to Misha and handed him the phone after telling Charlie to tell him what she thought. As soon as he was handed back the phone, Misha started telling them what was going to happen and why. Phillip put the phone to his ear again. "You more than likely just saved us a great deal of heartache. Thank you, love."

"I was only thinking about what Toby said. He wanted to bring them down, and I thought that this might be a way to do it." Phillip told her what they'd figured out about the credit cards and the returns. "I've run into that before. Not me doing it...let me think. The guy was arrested on credit card fraud. I guess he'd gotten a credit card in this other couple's name and had done that to them. He had...I think he timed it so that they'd never see the bill. You know, get the stuff bought then return it before they got the first bill. By then he'd turned in the stuff and gotten the cash. Not all places will do that, but he had enough, I guess, that he went away for a long time."

Phillip related the information to his brothers via their link. They'd not gone into the building as yet, but they were moving in that direction. Misha stopped them just as the door was opened and looked at him. He'd seen that look before...he was nervous.

"I need two people to go in and have a look around. Me and...who?" Everyone lifted their hands and he smiled. "I need someone to go in with me that can be shadowed. Anyone with that ability can go."

"How about Phillip and I can take the bottom floor? Then each of us can pair up with both Thomas and Linyah to go with them. That leaves three to cover the other exits in the event something goes wrong." Nic looked at Phillip as he continued. "You want to partner with me?"

Phillip nodded, knowing that Nic knew something or he would never have decided how they were to go in. He had a feeling that Misha knew it as well when he nodded at him and told him to be extra careful. Nic should, by all rights, have stayed behind with his father, but if he said he was going in, then he'd be going in with or without their help. As they jetted into the room, the first thing that hit him was the smell.

Dead. Phillip nodded at Nic and let Misha know what they'd run into. Misha said they could smell it as well. As they moved into the building, deeper into the confines of the walls, Phillip had a thought and reached for Nic just as he was going to open a door. *You see something?*

No. But if that door is rigged, don't you think we'd be better off bypassing it for safer ways in? Nic looked at the door, then put his bare hand on it. *Is there something there?*

Two men. Waiting. Phillip nodded but stood waiting. *Go through the door to the left of them, about five feet. Then I will go in the other direction. We should be able to take them out before they can us.*

It worked. Both of the men were dead before they even realized that Nic and he were there. As they made their way into the building, Phillip felt pretty good about this. They had no idea what was going to happen and were cautious about everything. For all they knew, this, too, could be a trap and they were going to be hurt. But they were ready should anything come up. Or at least he hoped so.

They saw the other men just as they rounded the last bend in the hall. There were about a dozen of them and they were dressed as Nic was, in full body armor, as well as armed. Nic told him to wait and while he did, he reached for Misha to tell him what they'd found. Misha said there was nothing on the upper floors and that they'd join them. In less time than it took for him to talk to his brother, ten of the guard that had come with them were lined up around the room, all of them darkened so that they couldn't be seen.

Just before the order was given for them to take the men, they shifted on their feet and Phillip could see the family. All five of them were sitting on the floor gagged and tied up, and behind each of them was a single man with a gun to their head. They were ready for anything as well, it seemed.

Now what to do? If the guard attacked, the people would be dead. If they took them out all at once, there was slightly less of a chance of the people being killed. Either way, blood would be shed.

Misha showing up gave them a working plan. They were going to stand just behind the family with the shadows of the room around them. Five of them for the five people. When the order was given, each of them would snatch up the person in front of them and disappear, leaving the guard that had more than likely taken them without hostages, and clearing the way for the guard from the castle. It was going to be tricky, but Misha said they could do it.

As soon as they moved to be where they needed to be, Phillip took a breath and let it out slowly. This was it, game time, and he needed to concentrate. But all he could think about was that they were missing something. Before he could figure that out, Misha said *now*, and he reached for the oldest teenager. Before he could think, he took him to the back of the building just as shots were fired inside.

CHAPTER 7

Charlie was at the airport when the jet touched down. She wanted to just hold Phillip. He'd told her several times that he was just fine but she needed to touch him, to see him to make sure he was really all right. As the stairs were taken to the door, she made her way to the plane with Maribel on her right. Hannah was on her left, and she was pretty sure that they looked like some sort of firing squad or something the way they were walking toward their men.

Misha was off first. The shirt he had on was still bloody, but she knew that he was all right as well. Hannah had told her several times that they were immortal, and as there were no blades there, they'd managed to keep their heads about them. Charlie was sure it was supposed to be a joke, but for the life of her, right now she didn't get it.

Rider was next, with Nildale, who had been shot. Phillip had told her how the man was more upset over his favorite shirt being ruined than being shot. One of the men that had been running from the building had taken aim and fired at Nildale before he could think to duck for cover. Sina was there at the bottom of the stairs even before he was finished coming down them. They both disappeared immediately.

Phillip was next, and Charlie felt her heart pound a little harder in her chest when she saw the blood on his shirt. As soon as he pulled her into his arms, she felt as if the entire world could go to hell. When he let her go, they were standing in a room that she'd never seen before.

"Our bedroom." She looked around again. "I wanted to surprise you, but now all I can think about is fucking you. Hard and fast."

There was a big bed in the room, made up, with pillows fluffed high on it. She moved to it, stripping off her clothing as she went. Dropping her blouse and bra on the floor, she toed off her shoes even as Phillip cupped her bare breasts from behind.

"Bend over for me." Doing as he wanted, her clothing was suddenly gone. Not torn from her as he usually did, but simply gone. She felt his naked cock at her pussy and moved back against him. "Christ, I have to do this. I'm so sorry."

Bending her at the waist so that her hands were on the bed, her ass in the air, Phillip slammed into her. It felt filling and a little painful, but oh so wonderful. Even as he pounded her, his hands at her hips gripping her hard enough that she knew she'd have marks, he never stopped. And when he leaned over her, his body pressing down on hers, his finger slid into her pussy and he gave her clit a hard twist, and she screamed out her release as he bit down hard on her shoulder.

Again. His voice, his command, echoed in her mind. It was as if he'd pushed a button on her body. She came hard, screaming out his name over and over again even as he tossed her on the bed, flipping her over as he did so. And when he turned into his cat, all she could think to do was run, but stopped when he commanded her to.

If you run now, he's going to run you down and hurt you. He's too needy, like I was, to have you play with him now. Give him what he wants and I promise you, you'll come harder than you ever have when I take you.

Nodding, she watched the huge leopard as he moved closer to her. His massive head was between her legs, his nose buried into her pussy so deeply that when he licked her, she felt it enter her. It was like being fucked and it felt amazing. As he licked her, his thick rough tongue setting off tremors all over her body, she cried out when he put his paws on her thighs and held her open for him.

He brought her five times in quick hard punches. Each time he made her come, licking her quick, his huge teeth gently nipping at her flesh, she knew that when he was finished, had his fill, Charlie was going to be nothing but a puddle of sated sex.

When Phillip stood up as himself, Charlie sat up on her elbows and looked at him. He was gorgeous, his body hard and muscled. The fur on his chest and arms was the same color as his groin, light with dark places that she knew was a part of his cat, and which gave him an untamed look, sexy and wild. As he fisted his cock, precum dripping in a long stream from his tip, she sat up more and reached for him. Phillip moaned loudly when she wrapped her hand around him.

"Can I drink from you?" He moaned again and she watched his face as his eyes darkened with need. "Your cat enjoyed my pussy. I've never been so relaxed before. Will it be like that if my cat licks your cock?"

She let the cat take her. While he'd been gone, Hannah had been helping her call to the big animal, showing her how to keep her calm and to bring her out to play, as she'd called it, when she wanted and not only when she was stressed. Phillip sat on the bed when she moved to the floor, her cat careful of the rugs beneath her feet.

"Lick me. Gently. Since you're not very— Holy Christ, yes."

Her mouth moved over his cock but she didn't bite him, though she was worried about nipping him. Instead, she tasted him, licked his balls and cock until he curled his hand into her fur and pulled her away. When she moved back, Charlie let her cat taste her mate again before she let her human come back to him. Charlie took Phillip into her mouth this time and sucked hard while cupping his balls. He came down her throat almost immediately.

As she crawled up on the bed beside him, he startled her when he pulled her over him and his cock. Reaching between them, she touched her fingers to the crown of him, circling the dark skin while she rode his body. Lifting herself up on her knees, she lowered herself over him while he held his cock. And when she was seated, he held her still until she looked into his face.

"I love you." She nodded, but he shook his head. "No. You don't understand. I really do love you. With all that I am. Not just because we're mated, though that is enough, but I love you. Am I making myself clear?"

"Yes. You love me more than anything. Just as I do you." Grinning, she looked around the room. "But really, where are we? Did you check to see if anyone was home before moving us to the closest bedroom?" She rode him slowly, and all he could do was moan, so it took him several seconds to answer her.

"It's ours. I made an offer on it a few weeks ago. Before I met you. I mean, I knew about you but hadn't met you yet. The decorators came in last week and set things up for us. Not all of the house, but this room and the kitchen." She rolled her hips again and asked him if he had the entire house ready for them. "It will still need some things. She said that the living room and dining room are ready for furniture, but the bathrooms will need to be…why are we talking about the house when you're riding my cock?"

Her body swayed then. Every part of her wanted to hurry through making him come, feeling his body release in her this way. But she took her time, rolling back and forth as she cupped her breasts and pulled on her nipples. When he sat up, her clit touched his groin, and she had to hold onto him while he held her to him and he suckled her breasts.

"Come for me, Charlie. Come on my cock so that I can take you again." Her movements became less smooth and more erratic. As she rode him faster, her body crying out for release, he rolled her to her back and settled between her thighs, pushing himself into her. "Come."

She did, her body bowing up off the bed nearly in half. Even as he leaned down then, taking just the tip of her breast into his mouth, Charlie curled her legs around his legs and moved with him, helping him bring her again and then again as he feasted on her breast. Then when he came, his cock buried so deep inside of her that she felt it at her throat, they came together, releasing hard and loudly. Then he leaned to her throat and bit her hard enough that she saw not just stars but rainbows and sparklers, even birds flying around her head. When he dropped on her, Charlie could only just lay there, her eyes closed and her body spent as her heart began to slow back to a normal beat.

"Christ, you've killed me." Charlie giggled and rolled with him when he moved to his back. "Anytime you want to ride me, you go right ahead. I don't think I've ever come that hard in all my life."

She sat up after about an hour, the lure of the house calling to her. When she pulled her shirt from the floor, Phillip sat up and leaned his head on his hand. She was dressed before he asked her where she was going.

"I want to see our house. Come on and see it with me. Or you can lay there…is there lots of room on the property? Because when this stupid thing with the book is done, I want to go back into business. I love that job."

He nodded and stood up. She couldn't find her shoes and she asked him where he'd tossed them.

"I didn't tear them off you. Just think of getting dressed and you will be." She cocked a brow at him, and he laughed at her. "Seriously. Watch."

She grabbed for the chair and held it while clothing seemed to just fade onto his skin. Boxer briefs were first, then socks and pants. As his shirt began to make its way over his body, she looked down at her own body and thought of her shoes and socks. Then she thought of the pretty boots she'd seen while with Hannah the other day, and the pretty blouse. Those two things appeared on her even as she thought of silk and sexy.

When Phillip growled low, her body caught fire and she looked at him. Every part of this man made her heart race and her body feel heated. When the rest of his clothing was over him, sadly, she turned to the door to leave. If there was ever a time when she needed a minute, this was it.

Charlie made her way to the stairs when she heard him laughing. She was nearly to the stairs when she heard a noise below them. Phillip came out of the room just as something crashed in one of the room's downstairs.

"Stay here." She nodded and backed from the stairs when he told her to. When Thomas appeared in the room beside his brother, Charlie put her hand over her mouth and tried to stifle a scream. If he was bringing in the troops, she was terrified all the more by it.

As the two of them made their way down the stairs, Charlie reached for Murph. Two days ago she had found out who the woman was related to, and knew somehow that the two of them were nothing alike. Charlie had never met Mr. Murphy, but she'd learned firsthand what he was capable of. And now that he was dead, she was no less afraid of what he could do to her, even from the grave.

I'm coming with Misha and Carter. We were coming back from the office and heard from Thomas. Just stay out of sight. She said that she would. *Even if you hear one of us, don't go down until someone comes for you, understand?*

Yes. I understand. But Phillip is down there with Thomas, and I know that Thomas can't get hurt, but Phillip is all that I have. She asked her what she meant. *Phillip isn't like you guys, right?*

Oh honey, we're all alike. Including you. Charlie started to ask her what she meant, but Murph spoke again. *We're outside. Just stay put.*

She heard the sound again, like something hard had hit the floor. Then she heard laughter. Charlie wasn't fooled by it. Someone down there could have been thrilled to death that they'd caught Phillip, her Phillip. But when someone else laughed, this time she knew it was Misha. And whatever was going on had her curious now. Moving slowly down the steps, she stopped when she saw Murph. The look on her face made Charlie smile.

"You had an intruder all right. Come on down and meet the rest of the family."

Charlie had no idea who she was talking about, but went down the rest of the stairs. The big man sitting on the floor nearly had her running again, but then he turned and looked at her. It was the wink that had her thinking it was safe to proceed. Good lord, was every man in Phillip's family able to lift cars without breaking a sweat?

"This is James Luna. He's the pack alpha and a good friend to the family. Apparently, he had no idea we were here until he...heard us." Charlie flushed hotly and then looked at Phillip when he laughed. "He was trying to get out before we noticed he was here, and he knocked over the vase on the stand over there. He was leaving us a housewarming gift."

Charlie looked at the broken vase, then back at the man. She noticed that while he was shirtless, he had a blanket wrapped around his waist. It occurred to her that he was naked. Blushing more, she turned to look at the large gift bag on the table. She walked over to it and pulled out the large soft blanket.

"Oh, this is beautiful." It was too. The colors were very earthy in that there were colors one would find in the woods...dark browns and reds, as well as golds and greens. When she took it to her cheek to see if it was as soft as it looked, she smiled at Phillip.

"My wife, Sandra, made it. She's been looming for years now. Mostly things like placemats and small rugs, but she wanted to make a blanket and this is what she got. I think she's got it in her head to make several more now. We'll be the warmest pack in all of the world when she's done." When she looked back at James, he was standing up, but the blanket that someone had given him was wrapped around him fully now. "If you don't mind, I'd like to bring my wife and son over soon to meet you. Phillip gave us permission to run here, and I want you to meet them before we scare you."

"Scare me?" He nodded, and she looked at Phillip before something occurred to her. Looking at James again, she smiled. "James is...Luna. That's moon. Pack. Wolves. You're wolf. You're the leader of the wolves around here, right?"

"Yes." He bowed low before standing again. "Thank you, my lady. You have made my entire day by not telling me that I wasn't worthy of your home. I'll return sometime. In the meantime, if you see wolf out and about, it's more than likely us. We've decided to aid the household in watching for the criminal types. I'm to understand that there are some...not so desirable people about."

"You have no idea." As she put the blanket down, she put out her hand to shake his. "I'm not sure how this works. But I have learned that touching hands will give us both something in return. Am I correct?"

"Yes. If I touch your skin to mine then smell it, your scent will forever be mine. And you will in turn be able to contact me, track me, as well as read my mind." She looked at Phillip, and he nodded. "You're new to this."

"Yes. In more ways than one." When James took her hand, she felt the connection immediately. And she could see that his wife was expecting their second child and that James was very happy. She could also feel his worry. "I'm sure that she will be just fine. And I'd love to have you guys come around. Anytime you wish."

As soon as he left, she went into the living room with the rest of the family that had come to her aid. She thought about having a large dinner in this house, and smiled at Murph when she came to sit beside her.

"You should know that they love to eat." Charlie just looked at her. "The dinner idea. I could see it working in your head. I can read your mind too, but I didn't. But I am hungry, and I'm pretty sure the rest of them would love to come and see the new house. I'll even have someone go and get Jackson to help you get the food ready. But you will need to get yourself a cook. It will be imperative to have someone here to protect you, as well as have all the supplies on hand in the event that we just show up out of the blue."

"I see. And this cook…will I need his help? Even if I was just thinking of steaks on the grill? I mean, I don't even know if I have a grill here or not." Murph said that there was one, that Misha had it in the back of his truck. And yes, she would always need a cook's help for a house this size. "Another housewarming gift, I take it?"

"Yep. And so you know, in addition to a cook, you'll need a staff. Not just for when we come over, which is a lot, but because you never know when one or all of us are going to get called away. And usually someone has to keep an eye on Max for me. He's my son. Max doesn't really need us to watch over him, but he's a great kid and needs to have someone around to keep him busy. He's a genius and bores easily."

Charlie had no idea why that one little boy would need staff around when he stayed with people, but she did ask if they wanted to stay for dinner. Charlie didn't even know if there was food in the house, but as soon as Linyah's mom and dad showed up with a tall man, things started to appear around the house. Charlie decided that this family could be very helpful and scary at the same time. As the rest of them arrived, all of them with bags of food, Charlie stood out of the way. She'd been alone for much of her life. Even when she'd lived with her parents, she'd spent as much time in her room as possible. It was a little overwhelming to have so many people in one place at one time. Then Hannah came to talk to her.

~~~

"This is Rocco. He's from the castle. And while I'm sure you have a handle on all sorts of stuff, Sina and Nildale have asked that you use him in your household. I guess he can cook like you've never tasted before, and he's here to keep you safe." Hannah watched Charlie's face and knew that the other woman was slightly nervous around her. All of them were, she supposed. What she didn't understand was why. A lot of them were way scarier than she was. "Rocco has magic that can keep —"

When Charlie raised up her hand, Hannah had to smile. She'd done that a lot, too, when she'd first come to this family, and there hadn't been as many of them then. As she waited for Charlie to get a grip, she looked around the large kitchen area.

It was bigger than theirs, hers and Misha's. And the refrigerator was bigger too. Wider than a side-by-side and taller as well. There were cabinets everywhere and she knew that, like hers had been, they'd be full of everything needed in a new home. As Rocco stood at the big butcher-block, directing the two women that had come with him that were helping with dinner, Hannah got up to brew some tea. And just where hers was at her own house, the tin was waiting for her.

"This house, all of this. Is it really ours? I mean, Phillip said it was, but I don't know if he was kidding or not. It's much bigger than we need, don't you think?"

Hannah looked around before answering Charlie. "Not really, when you think of this family. I mean, there were the six of them. Their mom, and then I came along. Now there are four women, including us, the rest of them as well as

Kendra, Nic, and their parents. Max is also added in, as well as the son I'm having. Then there are my mother and a few others that I'm sure I'm forgetting." Hannah handed her a cup of the tea that had become an everyday part of her routine, and sipped hers as Charlie absorbed this. "You should have seen us at Christmas. It was amazing. Everyone came to our house, and we opened presents for what seemed like hours. Then we ate. All day. It was the first Christmas that I'd ever had. Max too."

"I heard about your life." Hannah nodded. She had been embarrassed at first to know that so many had known about her horrific childhood, but not so much anymore. She was better now, not just in health but with love as well. "This is more than I ever thought would be mine. I mean, not just the healthy part, because that's really great, but being in love. With a leopard man."

"You're going to be just fine. I know it. But we do have to talk about some things. Misha asked me to talk to you while things are being put together in the other room. I guess that in addition to the couch, there was an entire truckload of things in the garage that Phillip had had his mom help him order for you guys. Furniture, as well as linens and things for the rest of the house."

Charlie nodded and played with her cup of tea. When Rocco put a tin of cookies in front of them, Charlie took one and stared at it as she sat there. Hannah waited. She'd been good at it before when she'd lived with her abusive so-called *mother*, and now she'd gotten really good at waiting until a person was ready.

"The book. Did you know about it? The one that got me into this mess in the first place?" Hannah told her that everyone knew about it, including the great wolf that roamed the property. "I guess that's what he meant when he said he was going to keep the criminal elements out. I'm guessing he means the men that are after the book."

"Yes. We have more information on that should you want it." Hannah watched as Charlie thought about her question. "You don't need all of it now, but I do want you to know that two men have been arrested in the last three days trying to hire someone to come and kill you. They'll never hurt you...well, maybe hurt you, but not kill you. You're an immortal like us."

"I think someone told me that before. I might have been a tad overwrought to have remembered it, but what do you mean by that? Immortals live forever. Is that what is going to happen to us?" Hannah told her it was. "And how do I...I don't know, is there a way to kill me? Us? I mean, I've read some books that talked about immortality, and there is always something to kill them off."

"Removing your head." Charlie nodded but said nothing. "You should know, too, that it's not as easy as it sounds. You have a great deal of magic on your side that will prevent that from happening. And there are certain things, rules, which have to be applied before someone can do it. There is only one kind of steel that would work, and it has to be a sword and nothing else. Kendra told me that a few weeks ago. There are other things that you can do as well. Magic that will help you in your everyday life."

"You mean like dressing without needing to go to my closet?" Hannah grinned and nodded. "What else can I do? I'm assuming that having clothing appear and disappear isn't going to keep someone from killing me."

"No, unless you use it to distract them. Then that will buy you some time. But you can shift too. Your cat is more powerful than a normal shifter cat. Not just because of you having this little extra, but because you're a part of the royal family. When Thomas married Linyah, the rest of us got their magic too. As well as part of the estates that the family owns. We're an extremely wealthy family." Charlie said she wasn't sure normal even came into the equation now. "You're probably right, but you can also hide in the open, blend in where no one can see you. Also, you can read minds. Most of the time we stay out of each other's heads, but there are times when it's necessary. Like when we can't find someone, we can search someone's head to see what they know. And the men use it to gather information about a job they're on. It's saved them a great deal of time and accidents being able to do that."

Charlie was calmer now but no less overwhelmed, Hannah could see that. While she was being told what everything was, Hannah knew also that in a few hours, when it hit her, Charlie was going to have a million questions. Rocco was moving food around to suit himself, which was good, and he only asked Charlie a couple of questions before he realized that he was in charge of this area. When she sat down again, Hannah watched her face.

"They're coming for me, aren't they? Not me, per se, but the book. I know you said that men were arrested in an attempt to come for it. There will be more, won't there?" Hannah nodded. "And if I said that I should go, lure them away from this family, you and your baby, I'd meet with resistance. Not just from Phillip, but I'm thinking the entire family."

"No." Charlie looked relieved for all of a second. "You'd not be able to leave with the intentions of luring them away. No one here would let you. We are family now, and we protect each other."

"But...." Hannah waited. "But I have not just these people after me, but that loony woman too. Sonya. I don't think she's going to just quit because Phillip and I are together, do you?"

"No, but I think Kendra is working on that one. Along with her staff. And I've not known her long, but I'm betting she's not one I'd want to fuck with when she's pissed off." Hannah knew there was more, but again she watched her new sister. "Charlie, you're going to be just fine. I know this. If they can protect me from the people in my former life, you're going to be just fine with us as well. And if, as you said, you know about it, then you understand when I say, these people, your family, is kick assed."

"So I keep hearing."

Charlie sat down, then stood up again. Hannah wanted to reach into her head and figure out what had her so stressed, and almost did before Maribel walked in the room. She moved around the kitchen like she'd spent her entire life in this one. And when Charlie got in her way, she told her to have a seat.

"Now. I'm your mother-in-law. Did you know that?" Hannah nearly laughed at the expression on Charlie's face, but one look from Maribel had her stopping that. "As I was saying. I'm your mother-in-law and I expect you to listen to me over everyone else. Including Phillip. He's my baby so I do tend to give him a little more wiggle room than I do the rest, but I wanted to talk to you. It's about your business."

"My business?" Charlie was clearly confused. Then when it hit her, she started shaking her head. "I don't know if I still have one or not. I've not been able to work it for some time now. Even if I did have a few orders, I'm pretty sure that the people who put them in are no longer interested. I'm more than likely bankrupt as well."

"Nonsense. You're going to be extremely successful. I'm sure that you're going to have some people that will be slightly upset, and they'll come around soon enough. But about the business. I was wondering if you get a discount on the things you buy. Like those pretty soaps and things I saw in one of the baskets online. By the way, you took some very good pictures of your things. I have a long list of things I want you to make me for the Memorial Ball that's in May. It's a big thing and I'm in charge of gifts for sponsors."

"I make those. Well, I make a lot of the little things in the baskets that I couldn't get wholesale." Both Hannah and Maribel looked at Charlie. "It really isn't that big of a deal. I looked up how to do it, got the stuff to do it, and there you go. It was cheaper than buying them. No one wants to have normal soaps, so to make a little extra money I started making some of the things in my baskets."

"Good heavens. What else? Please tell me you make those adorable little bears and things for the baby baskets. The ones that look like they're made from an old quilt?" Charlie nodded and looked decidedly embarrassed. "And those little washcloth animals? You make those too, don't you?"

"I try to make as many of those things myself as I can. Like I said, I needed to save money. And what I can't make on my own, I buy in bulk. There is still a lot of inventory in the barn out back of that house I lived in. I've been paying the rent on it, so I know that he hasn't sold it off." Maribel asked her if she'd made plans to build here to work. "Well, yeah, but I have to wait until this thing with the book is over. And the loony woman. Then I'll have to find me a place to work. I'll need something to put them together in, as well as a place that will be easy for pickup and deliveries."

"Oh honey, all of this will be done soon enough. The looney woman included. Sooner now that I'm involved." Charlie looked at Hannah and she could only shrug. "You'll see. In no time, this entire thing will be over and we can get to raiding your shelves. This is going to be so much fun. Why, I might even come and work with you. How much fun would that be?"

Hannah had to hide her smile. She was sure that Charlie was thinking the same thing she was. Maribel could be a force when she wanted, and Hannah had a feeling that she and Charlie were going to butt heads all the time if they tried working together. But she was right on one thing, Hannah was sure it was going to be fun.

CHAPTER 8

Dottie left a message at Lanning Search and Rescue for the third time. She had no idea how to get in touch with just Phillip, but she knew that they did work at the rescue place. She'd seen it on their shirts that first day and had looked up the number in the directory.

When she hung up the phone, she looked at her husband, who was sleeping still, and moved to the window of their drabby hotel room. Trying not to look at the day old donuts, she decided that if she never saw a donut or sweet roll again, it would be just fine with her. She stepped out of the room to see young Max leaning against their car. The young man looked as if he were harmless, but she knew better.

"How did you get here?" He looked at the taxi that was just pulling out of the lot. "You shouldn't have sent him on his way. I want you to go away and leave me alone. If you'd take a message to Phillip, I'd appreciate that, but I have nothing to say to you."

"I'm sorry, but I can't do that. I have to talk to you. And now is when it will have to be. Later will be too late." He nodded to the restaurant, and she wondered if he meant to feed her. The need for something not sweet made her

117

mouth water. "I'll buy you a meal or two and leave you something if you help me. But you will feel better once you've eaten a real meal. I don't want to have to hurt you, but if you don't let me talk to you.... Lives are at stake for what you've set in motion. Charlie doesn't deserve what you've done to her."

"I know."

He nodded once and led the way to the restaurant. Dottie thought about waking her husband, but knew that he'd not come or he'd take forever getting ready. She needed to eat now. And talking to this young man, she knew it was going to go a long way toward helping her with what they'd done.

As they entered the large open restaurant, she looked around. As much as she'd wanted to come here over the last several days, there had just not been any money for it. Instead, for the last week they'd been eating leftovers from the breakfast for each meal. It was too much. Food, something nutritious, was what she needed right now.

The coffee was brought first, and Max ordered himself a glass of unsweetened tea. She thought he was making fun of her, but as soon as she sipped the coffee, she knew a new kind of pleasure. As soon as the waitress took their order, Max put both his hands on the table and a woman appeared. It was Sonya. But even though she could see her, Dottie realized that she wasn't there with them. It was just an image of the woman she'd grown to hate over the last several days.

"She's the one that asked you to take care of Charlie. Am I right?" Dottie tried not to think about what else this kid could do, but nodded. He was scary, but for some reason she knew so long as she didn't try to run or do anything stupid, she'd be just fine. "I won't hurt you. But I have found out some things, now that you're no longer working for Sonya, that you should know."

"Like what?" The image moved again and there was her husband in a hospital bed with all kinds of tubes hooked up to him. She knew that this wasn't an image from long ago, but now. Or soon. "You know this for sure, or are you trying to scare me?"

"He's going to die soon without help. And you won't be able to help him, and Sonya won't. She's washed her hands of you. Not that she won't try to kill you both, but she won't help you. Either of you. His diabetes has returned, along with your cancer. You, too, only have weeks to live. You must have known this." Dottie nodded. She'd been having nose bleeds for the last two days and knew what that meant. And hiding it from Curtis was getting to be more and more difficult. "I'm sorry. If I could help you, I would."

"I know you would if it were possible, but I've made my bed, so to speak, and now I must lay in it. I figured out that she'd revoked our bargain several days ago, but I thank you for being honest with me. I even called Phillip this morning to tell him what I knew." Max nodded. "I see. That's how you found us?"

"No, I've known for a couple of days where you are. So do the rest of them. Not Charlie yet, but she will soon enough." Dottie nodded. She asked him if she hated her. "I don't think so. She's upset, but she doesn't hate you. But after what you've done to her and about her, you have to help her. She needs to get on with her life, and she won't if you continue to keep her from it. And you are. Just as surely as you are sitting here, you're keeping her from it."

"I wasn't a terrible mother to her. There were times, which I'll admit now, that I wished we'd not said yes to

119

taking her. But for the most part, I loved the girl. But that's neither here nor there. Sonya came to us almost twenty-four years ago. I was sick then too. The cancer in my head had spread to the rest of my body, and the doctor told me that it was fast moving and that I'd be dead within a month. Just as matter of fact as that. Then Curtis fell ill and I was ready to do one of those murder-suicide things when she knocked on my door." Dottie had never told anyone the next part before, but she knew that this was her only hope. "I often wondered as the years went by if she'd made us sick to get what she wanted. Money was good, but we had enough for the two of us. It was our health that was going to end us."

"Your husband was and still is a diabetic. His health, while poor, was not nearly as bad as you were led to believe it was. You, however, were healthy until then. There were no signs of cancer before that, so I believe you are correct in your thinking. It's the same thing that Nic and I thought when we started digging. She used you both." Dottie nodded, and when her food was set in front of her, she wasn't as hungry as she'd thought. "You must eat. I can't help you if you don't stay at least marginally healthy."

Dottie toyed with her food. It had sounded so good before this conversation. A hamburger and french fries, with all the trimmings. Dottie smiled a little then, remembering that this was Charlie's favorite meal, one she would order no matter where they had gone out to eat. She pushed it away in favor of getting this meeting over with.

"We were to keep Charlie for the rest of her life. There wasn't really any rules about how we were to raise her, but there were things she couldn't do. The one that sticks out in my mind more than anything was that she wasn't to date. That wasn't hard to keep under control, as she never seemed to mind staying at home on the weekends. And when she did go out, it was with her girlfriends, and there wasn't many of those either." Max nodded and asked her if she told her why they were to watch over her or why she couldn't date. "The dating part, she never said, only that it was necessary that she was kept from men. She was supposed to be something special. Not that I could see. I mean not really. I thought at first it meant that she had magic, like what cured us, but it was obvious that she was just as normal as I was. Maybe less so. Crafty but normal."

"And your husband, what did he think of taking her in?" She thought of her Curtis. "I know that he had some trouble with some of his employers. But what I want to know is, did he resent her in any way?"

"No. He loved her, too. I mean, it was really hard not to love her. She was a good girl. But if you mean trouble with his boss, I'm assuming you mean that you know that we were skimming the books. I know it was wrong, but we never took that much from any of them at one time. We did end up with millions of dollars, however. But we didn't spend it. It was for our rainy day." She thought of the plan and how it had gone to shit in a matter of days for them. "I didn't think he'd make it in prison, and I'm reasonably sure that he knew it, too. So from the start of us taking their money, we had a plan. I didn't want to lose him, and, like I said, he'd have never made it on the inside. Someone would have murdered him as surely as he would have been on the streets. He was going to die should he get caught or come close to getting caught, and then go away until I could join him. Fifteen years, we thought, was a good number of years for him to pretend he was dead. And the money would go a long way to keeping us safe. Fat lot of good that did us. Someone found out about our stash, and now we're broke."

"I know who has it." Dottie perked up, but he only shook his head. "It's not yours, and the people you stole it from aren't going to get it either. It will go a long way to helping people who need it. Medical expenses and other things like that. It's been set up as a charity fund, and it will be called Grant Works, after you and your husband."

There was no point in even begging him for it. She'd be dead; they'd both be dead soon enough. And even if Welshouse didn't find them, she knew that she'd be gone in a matter of weeks anyway. When Max spoke again, she had to ask him to repeat the question. "Where is she? Do you know where Sonya is now?"

"I don't know. I don't have a way of contacting her either." She looked at him and then at her plate. It took her several seconds to realize that she had eaten her lunch, every bite of it. "You did this? Why would you do something like that to me?"

"You need to keep your strength up. I only have a few more questions, but you're weak and you know it. All right?" At her nod, he continued. "I'm here about the book, too. Who have you told about it?" She'd hoped that no one would know that she'd sold Charlie out. They were desperate when she'd called in a few favors, and now she regretted it. "Dottie, who did you tell about it?"

"Welshouse. I think his first name is Gilbert or Ray, something. I can't remember exactly. He's the one that is mentioned in the first few pages of the book. And when I told him I knew where it was, he said he'd take care of me once he had the pages. I'm sure that what I think of as taking care of me and his way of thinking aren't the same. He's going to kill me, I know it." Max only nodded. Yes, she'd been thinking that was what Welshouse was going to do, but to have it confirmed was terrifying. "He said that when I got the book from Charlie...the pages, he kept calling them...he'd give me whatever I wanted. I'm not sure that I can do that to her now."

"He knows who she is and where you are. As of yesterday morning, there are three men watching you and your husband at all times." She looked around, and Max told her to relax. "They can't see us. I won't let them. But they are aware of where Charlie is, and soon they will make their presence known to us. Then he will die. But not before he tries to kill you and your husband first."

"What are you?" He smiled and told her. "And Doran, is that something I should know about? Are there more like you?"

"Yes." That was all he said, and it was enough to make her body stiffen in fear. "So long as you heed my warnings, you'll be safe where you are. Run or try to change the order of things as I've set up for you, and they will kill you. And no one will ever find your bodies. He means to cover his tracks, and there is a path that leads to you right up to the hotel room where you're staying."

Dottie wanted to beg him to save them. She knew that she'd done a lot of things wrong, hurt a great many people along the way, but she was different now. She supposed that staring death in the face, as she was, could change a person, but she truly did regret hurting Charlie. She knew that the boy, the one warning them to keep quiet and that made her eat her lunch, was going to be her last contact with Charlie.

"Will you tell her that I love her? Charlie, I mean, will you tell her that I'm sorry and that I love her so very much?" He said that he could do that. And what hurt her so much more than knowing that she was going to die was the fact that the boy hadn't told her that she could tell Charlie herself. It was that done of a deal.

He couldn't have been much more than fifteen, if that. Yet Dottie was terrified that even though he'd said that Welshouse would kill them, she knew it would be worse than that. They would suffer greatly for doing anything that this kid did not okay. And Charlie would be hurt as well. When he stood up, she watched as the waitress brought him a large bag and he handed it to her. She could smell the warm food in it and nearly sobbed, she was so grateful.

"Every day someone will come by your place, and he'll give you food and water. Don't go out of your room. If you do, there isn't any way for me to protect you. When he knocks on the door, you are to look out the peephole. He'll show you this." She look at the coin that he had in his hand. It was the face of a woman, beautifully chiseled out of gold. But what made it so much more unique was that it was in color...even the blue of the woman's eyes was there. "There are only five of these in the entire worlds. If he doesn't show you this, he doesn't work for my family. Understand?"

"All right. But what about the other men, the ones that are watching us?" Max told her that they'd never seen either of them since she'd opened the door and found him standing there. "Why can't you just take us someplace safe? I mean, please? I don't want to die."

"Because there is nowhere you'll be more safe than right here." The chill of his words made her bladder tighten up. "Go back and talk to your husband. Tell him what I've told you. And make him understand how important it is that you listen to what I've told you. If you leave the hotel room, you are as good as dead."

Even after he left her at the door, Dottie had questions. Most of them centered on whether they would live long enough for them to have food the next day. She knew that she wasn't going to live long, but it would have been nice to know just how long she had. Looking at her sweet husband, she didn't want to wake him but knew that it had to be done. As she set out the food, still hot from the restaurant, she had another thought. What if Sonya found them before Welshouse did?

Don't look for trouble that isn't at your doorstep. She wasn't surprised to hear the boy talk to her, wasn't even thrown off when he told her to remind her husband to stay indoors. Dottie was pretty sure that her life, short as it was going to be, was about as abnormal as it could get.

~~~

Phillip knew that things were coming to a head. He just wasn't sure what else he could do to calm things. There were so many things going on right now that he felt the pressure. Not a bad sort of pressure, because he knew that everything would turn out all right. But he was still a little nervous about things. And there were a great many things to choose from, too.

The book was first on his list of shit that could hit the fan. It wasn't talked about much and as far as he knew, no one had ever asked to see it. He'd never seen it, nor had Misha or the others. As far as he knew, the book was hidden away somewhere and safe. Or so he hoped. And if Welshouse and the others came to get it, he wasn't sure what to expect when asked to get it, and he had no idea where it was. He'd be shot, that much was a given. But as for the rest, who knew?

Then there was Sonya. Kendra was still looking for her and her band of men. She had them too, according to Toby, and when she hit the castle with all of them, a great many people were going to die. Not to mention, if she succeeded — and he'd yet to get a solid answer from anyone if that was possible — then he and his family were in trouble as well. He didn't want to think of how much destruction that someone magical could do to his family when they were just learning how to use their own magic.

Dottie was another concern. He knew that she'd been telling certain people, Welshouse included, that she had the book, or at least she knew where it was. Whether or not that was true, it was going to cause all of them problems if he came looking for it and she had lied. Not that he had any say in what happened to her, but he didn't want it to come down on the rest of them when she was caught without it. Phillip had a feeling that she'd give them up to save her own ass. Not that it would do her any good if it came to that.

"I talked to her." He looked up at Max, who had been coming over after classes to help out with some of the computer installations that he was having put in his and Charlie's new home. The kid was going to graduate soon, and Phillip was looking forward to going to the ceremony. "Dottie. I asked Mom and Carter and they said it was okay, so I went and talked to her. She's really down on her luck. Not that it's not her own doing, but she's hurting too."

"She and her husband are thieves, nothing more than that." Max said nothing. "I'm sorry. I'm a little...it's a lot. I was just thinking about it, and it seems that in order for us to have a normal life, we're going to have to do something. And soon. I'm just not sure what it would be."

"Define normal." Phillip nodded. It wasn't exactly normal in anyone's terms around here lately. "She isn't any better off than you or Charlie. And so you know, she regrets hurting her too. But I think there is more to this than just the book and Welshouse. Sonya did things to them…horrific things even now are being done to them that will kill them both. She preyed on their health issues. And Uncle Nic and I think she might have made them ill to the point where they were desperate for help."

"How so?" Max told him what he'd been able to find out, and then what was going on now. "That was nice of you to make sure that they have food. I'm sure…we need to get someone in there that can help them if they need it. Does this guy, Curtis…does he need insulin?"

"He should have it, but he won't use it. He believes that he is cured, and no matter what is told to him or, for that matter, how sick he gets, he thinks he's just fine. I think you'd call that having your head up your…butt. But I can ask Aunt Kendra if she has any medical personnel that can go in. A regular doctor might tell on them." Max apparently didn't have any more faith in humans than he did. "Also, I have someone watching over them. Two guards from the castle, so that if anything comes after them, and I'm sure they will, someone is there to defend them."

"I've done the same with Welshouse. I'm to be informed if he comes this way. I have a feeling he's going to sooner or later. That book means a great deal to a lot of people, I think." Max nodded and leaned back from the computer he was working with. When he turned in his direction, it took Phillip a few seconds to figure out what he was looking at. "Where is this?"

The camera was looking into a back yard. The reason he knew it was the back of someone's property was because he could see the pool and the pool house just to the right of the lens. Five people were there, and they looked to be talking, arguing about something, when a gun was brought out and four of the men were dead. The only one left standing was the one holding the gun.

"It's the Welshouse house. I don't know who they were, but I can only assume that it's him." Phillip nodded, but watched as a few people came out and started gathering up the bodies of the dead. "This was taken a few days ago, and those men were ones that he sent to find Charlie and the book. They failed him. This camera wasn't set up by me but the police. They had surveillance on the house twenty-four seven. However…."

Phillip looked at Max as understanding came over him. "However, it does them little good if the people watching the cameras aren't telling anyone what they see." Max nodded. "Christ. Is anyone honest anymore?"

"I'm beginning to think not." Max got up and went to the cabinet and took down two glasses as he continued. "There is more. Are you ready for it?"

"No." Max didn't say anything but continued to pour tea for them both. Rocco had gone to see about setting up a home delivery of groceries weekly, and Charlie was with Hannah and his mom, figuring out what else they needed for the house. "What else is there?"

"Welshouse is already in the area. He's been here since early yesterday morning. Whoever you had watching him is now on his payroll and you aren't getting the truth. I would suggest that you be on your toes from now on." Phillip reached for James, who had his men walking the area, and let him know to keep a sharper eye out. He told him that he was on it. "Also, Sonya is here, in this area, and her troops are not as many as she's led others to believe. However, they are magical, but nothing compared to the family. She's coming here in two days. And when she does, unless we're very prepared for her, people, this family...not all of them will survive it."

"Who? Can you tell me who gets hurt?" Max didn't answer, and that scared him a great deal. "How do we get prepared? I'm assuming that you know how this is going to end."

"Not entirely. I know what one outcome will be. But that is without us doing anything to get ready. And since I know that's not going to happen, let's just say that what I know stems on the idea that has us not getting ready for her." It was confusing, but he thought he understood.

Phillip got up to look for something to eat. It wasn't like him to eat when he was nervous, but right now he needed something sweet. He was able to unearth a box of cookies, not homemade, and set them between the two of them. After one bite, Max put his on the table, and it took Phillip two before he decided that they weren't fit to eat. Max told him he had a favor to ask.

"Anything. You know that. I don't know what I have that you need, but it's yours. You and your mom are making Carter so happy I feel like I could give you a blank check and it wouldn't be enough."

Max smiled and pretended to consider it before he spoke again. "Nothing like that. But I can't buy a building." Phillip asked him why not. "I'm not eighteen and won't be for six more years. I have the plans, but I need space. There is this building downtown that I'd like to purchase. It's perfect for what I want it for. And if it's all the same to you, I'd rather not tell you just yet what I want it for."

"All right. What do you want me to do? Buy it for you?" Max nodded. "I can do that. Have you seen it? I mean, all of it?"

"I have. They have an online showing of it, and I've looked it over a few times. Also, I've gone by it a few times on my way home from class and sort of snuck inside." He'd bet anything that Max knew more about the building than the owners did. "Will you? I know you have to talk to Mom and all, but she won't care. And she already knows, anyway, that I was going to ask, and while like you, she doesn't know what I need it for, she said it was all right with her."

"I do have to ask. Not that I don't believe you, but I still want to ask. She might...well, you know your mom. She can be a bit on the protective side when it comes to you." Max nodded and grinned. "How do you plan to make the payments for this place? I'm assuming you know how much it's going to cost."

"Oh yes. And I have the money for it now." He told Phillip how much he had. "The building is part of the revamp downtown project, and they are selling the buildings cheap. Then you have one year to have a business in it and hire out ten people to work it. That won't be a problem. Not for what I want it for anyway. You should invest. It's a good deal, and you can get a return on it almost immediately after you get a business in the buildings."

He asked him more about the buildings and which other ones he would recommend. Max had a list of four other buildings, and Phillip decided to see about getting them for himself. He didn't really need the money, but it would help the downtown area and him as well. A project other than going out on rescues. He was seriously going to have to talk to Misha and the others about the other job. He wasn't really enjoying it as much as he used to.

Max left just after one, but not before nearly cleaning out his cabinets of food. Growing boys, he'd told him, needed lots of calories. Not that Phillip cared. The computers were set up, and he had a direct line to the office computers as well should he want to work from home. Now he would be able to work here if he wanted and still get things caught up. Lately, especially since Charlie had come into his life, he'd been staying at home more and more.

When Rocco came in, he looked pleased with himself. Apparently not only had he been able to set up the grocery store deliveries, but he'd been able to hire a few more staff. The house really was too big for them, he supposed, but he did love it. Going out on the deck, he waited for the man to join him. Rocco said he had more news about Sonya.

"She has not been seen around her home, my lord. But there are others who have come across her. One such man—his wife is most unhappy with his hanging out with the woman—is said to have been spending nights there. He claims they are working, but he has been...the missus believes that she is beating the man. Did you know that Sonya has been in trouble with her magic for some years now?" Phillip said that Kendra had told him that. "Very good. And her army is based at the open field not far from here. Have it on good authority that she has as few as ten. The number is lessening daily because they are simply dying or running away."

That sort of confirmed what Max had said. She had few working with her, but they were magical. He asked him how good his source was. He grinned and said that a mad wife revealed so much.

"So she's ratting her husband out with Sonya." Rocco nodded. "Max said that she was going to attack the castle soon. Do you have any information on that?"

"No, but I will endeavor to find out. The queen, I hold her in high regard, my lord, and would do anything for her family." Phillip nodded and sat down after Rocco said he was going to start dinner.

He contacted Misha and let him know what he'd found out. Misha, of course, was concerned about Hannah more than the castle, which was the way it should have been. Hannah was having his child soon, and Phillip knew that he'd do just about anything to protect her as well. Including giving up his life.

You have a few visitors. And I say that only because they are not invited. Or so I'm assuming. James touched his mind not seconds after he closed the connection with Misha, and Phillip sat up straighter in his chair. *If I'm correct, and my wife seems to think that isn't as often as I let others believe, it's your man after the book. My people are watching his troops, but you have no worry about them.*

You've killed them? James told him not as of yet, but they would more than likely be dead before too long. *Where is Welshouse now? I mean, he's on the property then?*

One of those big monster four wheel drive things that men buy when they have no dick to speak of is coming up your drive now. I'm sorry about your guy in the gate house. He was gone before we knew they were on the property. He'd had no idea that he'd had anyone in the gatehouse, but thanked James for letting him know. *He should be there soon. I'm contacting your brothers and the rest of the gang. I have also taken it upon myself to let that guy in your kitchen know. He is currently recording everything that is going on. Just to be on the safe side.*

When he heard the car pull in the drive, he didn't bother moving. He'd wanted Charlie to join him on a run and was actually looking forward to it. But the man that cleared his throat had Phillip leaning back in his chair again and trying his best to look as if he had not a single care in the world. The gun pointed at him made Phillip stand up and lift his hands up with his palms out. Not that he was scared of getting shot, but he was pretty sure this man knew just how to kill him, thanks to Dottie.

CHAPTER 9

Ray told the younger man to have a seat. When he only stood there, staring at him, Ray told him who he was. He waited for the begging and was extremely disappointed when it didn't happen.

"I know who you are, Welshouse. And you don't scare me." Which Ray could see that he did not. "How did you get past the guard? And so you know, if you hurt him, there will be hell to pay."

"I'm afraid that he's dead." Young Lanning nodded, and Ray had a touch of fear. There was anger there, much more for the fact that he'd killed his man than him holding a gun on him. "Your roommate has something that belongs to me. I have come to retrieve it."

"My wife." Ray knew that, of course, but wanted to rile the man. Nothing was working on that end, and it took him a few minutes to realize that the man really wasn't impressed. "And what is it you think she has of yours? I'm pretty sure that when I brought her here, all she had were her things."

"Let's not play around, shall we? I have things I must get back to, and this is not helping your cause. You do know that I have the upper hand, don't you?" Phillip asked him how he figured that. "The gun, for one thing. And the fact that I've come prepared to take on your family if need be. I never come to one of these things alone. You will not get any help from anyone until I say so."

"Yeah, about that. You came with six men, and four of them are already dead. My friends and family are a little bigger than yours, and a good deal meaner." That startled Ray, and he was afraid that the man could see it. "What else do you have? Oh, and the gun? Not really a factor in this. I'm sure you have no idea what you're dealing with, and unless you have another gun somewhere on your person, that's not going to do you shit. There are rules of engagement with my kind, and you didn't even come close to being as prepared as you might have thought you were."

"What do you mean?" Ray leaned against the railing to steady himself. This man was much too confident and he didn't care for it. As far as his men were concerned, there was no way that he'd been able to take care of four of them already. They were trained by the best. Warfare was nothing to them, as they could kill a man with their bare hands, just as he could. Ray was sure the man was lying. A good guess on the number of men, but there wasn't any way he had people on the property that could outwit or out maneuver his men.

"What I mean is...."

Phillip sat down and leaned back in the chair. When he propped his feet up on the railing, Ray felt his temper move up. He prided himself on the control he had over himself, and this man wasn't going to win out. He mentally counted to ten once, then twice, then again before letting out a slow, long breath that he felt the man could hear. Things were not going as he'd planned. Fear was an emotion he enjoyed as long as he wasn't the one feeling it.

"What I mean is, you can shoot me full of holes, but it will do you little good. But if you don't mind me asking, since when do big leaguers like you come to do your own dirty work? I mean, don't you have minions for this sort of thing? Or do you like getting your hands dirty?"

"My minions, as you called them, are there to make my job easier. No one would dare interrupt me when I'm…what did you call it? Oh yes, getting my hands dirty. But I have discovered that if you want a job done right the first time, you never send in minions to do it for you. It's something that my father taught me." Phillip nodded and smiled. Ray had to let out a slow, even breath again, trying his best to control the hold on his temper that was slowly deteriorating. "What if I told you that I have your wife and that she's tied up in one of my many locations right now?"

"You don't." Ray finally had to sit down. If he didn't, he was going to shoot this kid and leave the book behind. His temper had never been so tested before. "If you had her, you would have started off with that. Besides, I'm pretty sure that if you did try to take her, one of the people she's with would have killed you. Or she would have. I'm not sure if you've ever met my wife, but she can be vicious when she needs to be. Killer instinct and all. And since that didn't happen, well, you're lying again."

Ray didn't even bother with that line of reasoning. He didn't have her, and he was pissed the man didn't believe him. What's more, he was sure the man was not going to do a damned thing for him.

Then Ray turned when he heard a low growl. Whatever he had expected, staring at the biggest leopard he'd ever seen was not even close to the list of shit that he had in his head.

"That would be my brother, Rider. Misha is the cat behind him, and the others are around the property looking for...wait, nope, they found your men, all of them, and are on their way here. I do think that Misha might be a tad pissy because he wasn't able to take care of your minions, but our good friend and wolf, he took care of them for us. Good guy James...you'd do well not to piss him off either. More than you already have, anyway." Ray didn't know what to do. In fact, he was pretty sure if he did anything, the cat was going to tear his throat out. When the cat moved one more step in his direction, Ray thought he was going to soil himself. "You should put the gun down now and sit your ass on the floor. The chair isn't working for them."

He did it. Ray wasn't sure how he'd sat down so quickly, but found himself staring into the big teeth of the biggest leopard he'd ever seen. And Phillip had his gun on the table in front of him. It was...he had no idea what to think about any of this but he was terrified.

"Now, we're going to talk and you're going to answer me. If you lie to me about anything, Rider is going to eat a part of you. Show him, Rider." The big cat moved to his foot and put his massive mouth over it. He was biting down when Ray realized he was really going to do it.

"Don't. For Christ's sake, don't do it. Please don't eat my foot." The cat looked at Phillip but didn't let him go. "I'll tell you whatever you want to know. But please have him let me go. I won't lie. I'll tell you everything."

The other cat, this one monstrous compared to the other one, just sat down next to him. Ray had a feeling that he was being sized up. The cat was actually looking at his throat to see if he could snap his jaws around him and take off his head. Phillip laughed, and he looked at him.

"You should know that I can also read your mind. I should have said that earlier, but I had to stall long enough for my family to come here. And also, your men aren't really dead, but they aren't going anywhere. The police will be called in a bit and then you all will go off merrily to jail. And if you tell them what has happened here today, you're going to be locked up with a big man named Bert. And Bert will make you...well, I hope you've registered somewhere for wedding gifts." When Phillip sat up in his chair again, Ray whimpered. "I'm not going to hurt you. They might, but I'm not. Like I said, I want to talk to you. For now."

"How did you train those cats to do as you wanted? There is no way I'm going to believe that they're men." Phillip only nodded and said nothing. "You have the upper hand now, but you won't always. I'm a man with great resources. As for this Bert person, if I ever see the inside of a prison, which I will not, then no one will dare touch me."

"You keep telling yourself that, if it makes you sleep better. And as for having the upper hand, I'm the man with the cats. And the book and gun. What is it about this book that would have you risk your life to come after it? I mean, there is a lot of code in it from what I understand, but not much in the way of information." Ray had seen several pages of the book. And he knew the kid was lying to him. "Ah, so Dottie sent you some of it. Oh well, I tried. But you should know that you're not the only one that thinks to come here for the book and kill my family."

"But I'm the one that is going to get it." The big cat at his head yawned, and Ray felt his balls tighten to his body. Christ, those teeth had to be three inches long and sharp as razors. "Tell them to back the fuck off."

Instead of doing that, the big cat laid his head on his lap. Ray knew that he had understood him and when he stretched out his paws, claws as big as his hand seemed to sprout from the ends. Ray closed his eyes and tried to think his way out of this. He wasn't sure there was a way out when Phillip spoke again.

"Misha said that if you piss on him he's going to be very mad at you. And I've seen him pissy. It's not something that I'd want to see again. Especially since you're just a human. Now, back to the book and what it means to you." Ray wanted to get up and kill the lot of them. The leopard put his paw on his thigh, and Ray felt the claws bite deeply into his flesh. "He said to answer me or lose the leg."

"I owed Murphy a few favors. Big ones that he was to collect on in the future. He told me about the book once. How it had all the information that anyone would ever need to bring not just me down, but hundreds of men just like me. When I heard about his death and that there was no mention of the book, I thought about collecting it, but had no idea who had it or where the bastard had even kept it. Then I heard from Dottie." The cats seemed to stand up as one, and he felt his bladder loosen just a little. Ray looked at the beautiful woman as she came onto the deck, and wondered what the fuck she was going to do to him.

"Hello, Ray." He nodded, not sure who the hell she was, but nearly knocked himself out when she reached out and tosseled his hair. "I'm Charleston Lanning."

"So?" The big cat growled at him, and when the woman went to sit on the lap of Phillip, something nudged at his mind. "Charleston Grant? You're a man."

"Obviously not." He moved to slap her, and the cat growled again. "Misha is pissed off enough. If I were you, I'd just sit still until the police get here. They have a few questions too. Like who is responsible for our man at the gate. Someone—I'm assuming it was you, or you know who did it—killed him. Shame on you for that. Did you think perhaps maybe asking to come up would have been nicer?"

Ray wasn't worried about the cops. He was glad now that he'd made a little side trip before coming here, and talked to the head man in the courthouse. Ray had the entire police department of this podunk town in his pocket. And a lot of the Feds, too, that were close. A single phone call and he'd be a free man. It was amazing how a little money could be flashed around in these small towns and still get you what you wanted. When Charleston laughed, he smiled at her as well. Having things set gave him the confidence that he should have had all along.

"You have fucked with the wrong man, Lanning. I mean, you don't think I got this far in my business dealings by being stupid enough to let one family and a backwater kind of police force get in my way, do you? Sure, you have the cats and my gun, but what else do you have? Nothing. Maybe you can get me on trespassing and carrying a gun, but nothing more. Neither of you were harmed. The man in the gatehouse, he was dead when I got here. I only came here to...to warn you of his death. As for the men you claim to have? Not mine. I have no idea what you're talking about. Arrest them, I don't really care." Phillip said nothing but held his wife. "When I'm finished here, you're going to regret ever knowing me."

"I already do. And so you know, the backwater police, as you've called them, aren't the only ones coming here. There are some Feds, but none that you have paid off. And thank you for that, by the way. That list of names you have in your head is going to go a long way to cleaning up that office too." Phillip listed two of the men that Ray had just recently spoken to, and Ray knew that he was fucked and tried his best not to show it. "You really are fucked, Ray. So badly have I wanted to see you rot in a prison cell, I never thought how happy I'd be to know that you'll never see the inside of one."

"Do you think you can kill me?" Phillip shook his head. "Yeah, I thought not. I'm a bigger man than you are, kid, and as I said, when I get out of this, and never doubt that I will, you are going to pay. All of you."

He heard the crunch of gravel in the driveway but didn't move, not that he could as yet. He either knew the men coming or not. Either way, he wasn't going to go anywhere but to his plane to regroup and to plan their deaths. And die they would.

As soon as the first man came around the corner, he felt better. A face he knew. But when he was shoved to the floor where he was, Ray noticed the cuffs at his back. The next two men he'd never met before. This was not going to go well after all.

"Raymond Welshouse? You're under arrest for attempted murder, murder, carrying a gun—"

Ray had to think quickly and knew that what he had in his head was the only thing that could save his ass. "I'd like to make a deal." No one moved in his direction as Phillip shook hands with the men in suits. No one, it seemed, cared one bit for anything he might have to say. "I know some things that you're going to want to hear. I can give it all to you for a price. My freedom and a promise not to bother these people again. You have my word on it."

"Your word means shit, so you know. And we already know about the shipments, the drugs, and all the money you have stashed away in your house. By the time we got to your house this morning…well, let's just say that the staff you had working for you was more than willing to tell us everything you know. You should do a better background check next time, if there is one, Ray. A couple of those people working for you, work for me. Nice that, you letting them gather all the information we needed to make this stick. You—and this thrills me to no end to say—you are going away for a very long time." Ray asked the man in the suit how that was possible. "Well, boy, it's because we had a tip a few days ago that you just might try something stupid like this. Misha Lanning and his family knew you'd be here, and damned if they weren't right on the money."

Ray was screaming about what he knew all the way to the car. When he was shoved in the back seat, another man was suddenly right there beside him. He had no idea who this person was, but the fact that he wasn't cuffed had him thinking he was with the cops.

"What the fuck are you doing here? I demand that you get out of here unless you're going to help me. And right now, I could use someone helping me. These people are going to pay." The man only nodded, and Ray noticed how he was dressed. "How the hell do you get in and out of that thing? Is it plastic? What the fuck are you doing here if not to help me out?"

"No. Body armor. It's very helpful when I have work to do. Like now. I'm here to take care of you. As you were told, Ray, you are never going to see the inside of a cell. And I'm going to make sure you don't."

Ray started to scream, but stopped when he felt the slice across his throat. As the man got out of the car...sort of disappeared...Ray tried to get someone, anyone to listen to him as he pounded on the window. The blood staining his view as he got weaker and weaker was his, and no matter how tightly he held onto his wound, it would not stop bleeding. No one, it seemed, really did care what happened to him.

~~~

Misha had gone in to dress, as had the others, but Phillip had stayed where he was and hadn't ventured around to the cars at all. He was pretty sure that he knew what had happened out there, but didn't want to go there to see. He looked at Murph when she sat across from him, handing him a large glass of amber liquid. Phillip took it but didn't say anything.

"You want it straight up or a little at a time?" He told her a little for right now. She nodded. "He's dead. Nic sliced his throat open and made sure no one found him until he was dead. Better that way for all of us."

"That wasn't really a little, now was it?" Her grin had him leaning back in his chair. "He actually brought men here to kill us. Just come up on my deck and put a bullet in my head. If I hadn't gotten a warning from James, I would have...what the fuck, Murph? I don't think he'd figured out that we were shifters, but someone would have told him eventually. The man...he would have gotten away with it too."

"Yes, he would have. There are just too many people on his payroll for him to get what he deserved. It had to be done." Phillip had already figured that out when the first five names in Ray's head were all federal agents he had on his side. "If we hadn't killed him, like you said, we'd all be hurting. And always looking over our shoulder."

"Charlie is going to hand the book over to them...the good guys, not the ones on his payroll. She said that she didn't want it here anymore, and she thought perhaps if it was out that they had it and not her, things would go easier for us all. I think she's right. Did you know where she had it?" Murph told him she'd not heard where it had been, only that Charlie had it here. "It was in the kitchen with a cookbook dust cover around it. I mean...Christ, anyone could have found it."

"But they didn't, and to be honest, I doubt that anyone would have even thought to look there. In a safe or even hidden in the yard, but not out in the open like she had it. That was brilliant of her." Phillip nodded. "There's more. Are you ready for it?"

"This has to end, Murph. Please tell me that sometime soon we all can just live our lives in a very quiet and normal way." He thought of Max asking him to define normal and smiled. "I'm not sure if I know what the word normal means any more. It's been so topsy turvy for a long time."

"I can give you some highlights if you want them. They're the good things that come our way." He nodded at her. "You have three children. A set of boy twins and a daughter. You have more children, but those will come first. Misha and Hannah will have their son and then several more after that. Those children grow up to run one of the biggest leaps there has ever been. Your children will be helpful in ways that will make it a safe haven, as well as a place that people will respect and grow old in."

"And you? What about you and Carter? The rest of the family?" She told him that was for another time. "Three children, huh? I like that. I guess this house isn't too big for us after all."

"No, it's not. Anyway, the rest." She handed him a file, something he'd not noticed until then. "Curtis Grant was killed this morning. Just after Max went to talk to them. He didn't stay in the hotel room and it got him killed. Dottie was hurt as well, but it was thought that she was going to

145

make it. When she got to the hospital this morning after she was hurt, they found that she had advanced ovarian cancer and has had it for a number of years. They only gave her a few weeks to live. Less I'm thinking from the reports. Not that it matters now. Someone got into her hospital room, even with a guard out front, and killed her as well. Made her pay, too, from the looks of it."

He looked at the pictures t in the file. Curtis had been shot several times and then he'd been marked. Someone had cut his throat, then pulled his tongue out of the large gaping hole. But what had been done to Dottie was much worse. She'd been burned and nearly cut from sternum to navel before her heart had simply given out. Phillip asked her if Charlie knew yet.

"No. Not yet. I can tell her, but you should be there." He told her that he'd tell her, but handed her back the pictures. "Dottie had given up everyone she knew. Apparently, she and Curtis had worked on their own book of names, and she had a list of them to give the officer that was first on the scene. He was one of the few good guys that are on the force. And as of this morning, I've taken the job as sheriff. Misha said it was the only way to make sure that everyone was safe. I don't know how much safer I can keep people, but I told him I'd do it until they voted me out come the next election."

He nodded and agreed with Misha. Murph was perfect for the job. And as much as she seemed to think that this was a temporary position, he knew that once she got in the office, they'd never let her leave. She'd not just clean it up there, but she'd have a better handle on what was going on with all the men too. Her abilities as Doran were going to help her in ways that would keep everyone on the straight and narrow.

"What else? I'm sure you know more than just that."
She nodded but didn't say anything. "Come on, Murph, I
can take it."

"They want to take Charlie in." He stood up, then sat
again. Phillip was not going to let anyone take her without
him. "Phillip, we're not going to let them, but they might be
able to do so without our helping them. As it is right now,
she's only going in for questioning. Nothing else. There are
too many players in this to have her out free. At least with
them, and you with her, she will be safe for a time. And
they can make sure that everyone knows she knew nothing
other than the book was in code that she couldn't read it."

"They think she had something to do with this? With
all these deaths?" She only stared at him. "What are you not
telling me? Damn it, Murph, just tell me."

"Sonya." That alone was almost enough to bring chills
to his body, but he waited for her to finish. "She's got the
ear of a few people, and she's telling them that Charlie was
blackmailing my dad and was a part of the entire ring. Not
that many are believing her, but she's using something on
them to get them to see things that aren't there. Such as,
there are some that think that Charlie was there when
her...when Dottie and Curtis were killed, and that she
actually pulled the trigger."

"You know that's not true." Murph told him that she
did know that. "So, just on that, a perfect stranger's word,
they're going to accuse her of killing the only parents she
knew?"

"It's because of that reason. They weren't her parents,
and when she found out, she went a little over the edge."
Phillip wanted to go and find Charlie but stayed where he
was. Getting as much information as he could was going to
help them, and he knew it. "Charlie isn't talking either. I

mean, she's handed over the book, but now she's just sitting there. I'm very proud of her by the way. She has it down. Never play poker with her."

He wanted to run screaming into the woods. Jokes. She was making jokes. But when he saw Charlie coming out of their house, he stood up to go to her. The men that had put Ray in the cruiser were just finding the dead man, and all hell had temporarily broken loose. Phillip held onto Charlie when Murph moved to take things under control.

"They asked me what I knew of Dottie and Curtis being killed. I think…they think I had something to do with it." Phillip told her that it wasn't going to stick. "But they want me to go downtown with them. I'm not going without a lawyer. Or someone bigger than them. Do you think you could ride there with me as your leopard? I'd pay him back with sex. He loves having sex with me, and I'd very much like to know I was safe. Wouldn't you?"

He laughed. With all the stress of the day and everything else going on, he laughed. When she smiled at him, he pulled her to his body and held her tightly, and wondered not for the first time how he'd ever made it before she'd come into his life. He knew that while it had been a little less chaotic, it was also boring.

"I'm going to go with Murph in a bit. Did you know about Curtis and Dottie?" He told her that he'd just found out too. "I was mad at them, but I didn't hate them enough to kill them."

"I'm going with you when they take you in. Murph said for now it's just for questions, but I'm going to be there with you. And I'm going to find us a good lawyer too. There is no reason for us to go into this half blind or halfcocked."

They both watched as an ambulance came and pulled Welshouse from the back of the car. People were looking for clues, but he knew that they'd never find any. Nic would never be charged with anything because he'd bet anything there wasn't a single shred of evidence tying him to the death. It would look like someone had gotten in and cut his throat, and it would never be tied to anyone in his family. The cameras on the other cars would prove that.

The questioning never happened. Sina showed up at the station with his mom, and everyone seemed to be going out of their way to make sure the two women were well taken care of. Someone had even taken a cruiser to his brother's house and brought back his mom's favorite cup so that she could have her tea in it.

But as for Charlie being questioned? No one, not a single person, could find any reason why she'd been brought in. When Sina winked at him, he knew that she'd changed their minds. He wondered if anyone realized what a wonderful person she was. His mom came over to him and kissed him on the cheek and told him that she loved him. Phillip thought things might just be looking up as they traveled to his home and they were both let out of the car.

For the first time in a while, they were alone at the house. It had been nearly six when the police and the rest of the department left them. The car had been put on a dolly and taken away about an hour before they'd gotten back, and the police, still trying to figure out how the hell anyone had gotten in the car without being seen, were now long gone too. Phillip was sitting on the deck with Charlie when Rocco came out to ask them what they wanted to do about dinner.

"I think I'll take my lovely wife out for dinner. I have a couple of errands to do in town anyway. Why don't you

join us, Rocco? It would be great to have you eat with us."
He, of course, declined, but told them that was an excellent
idea.

They were moving to the car to leave when Misha and
Hannah pulled in the drive. After inviting them to join
them, they were making their way into town and the
restaurant when Phillip remembered the buildings Max
had spoken of. Making a few phone calls while Charlie
drove, he made an offer on all four of the buildings on the
same block, as well as the one that Max had wanted him to
buy. He was feeling pretty good about things as they were
seated in the back of the restaurant. Phillip told Misha what
he'd just done.

As they talked over the restoration of the buildings and
what he might be doing with them, he saw Hannah rub her
hand over her belly. Phillip had a blinding moment of
clarity when he realized that he was going to be a father. He
was going to be a father sometime soon, of two boys and a
girl. For several moments he didn't think he breathed, and
when he did, he felt panicky. Looking at his brother, he
blurted out the first thing that popped into his head.

"How the hell do you be a good father?" Of course they
all laughed at him, and Phillip was okay with that. For now.
But to be a father, he was going to make sure that he took
notes on what Misha did and try his best to not be their
dad. Misha wasn't just his big brother and someone that he
looked up to. He was his hero and had been his entire life.

The only person that Phillip admired more than his
brother was his mom. Maribel Lanning was the best there
was, hands down. She'd pretty much raised them on her
own, gave them whatever they needed and not necessarily
what they wanted, and made them into the men that they
were. Good men. Not at all like their father. Yes, Phillip

thought, not being his sire was going to be a good start to being a great father.

CHAPTER 10

Sonya watched her men work. Most of them were failing at fighting, but their magic would more than make up for it, she knew. To have them at her side when she went to the castle was going to win the war for her. And when she was inside, she was going to use all her considerable powers to take the royal family down and set herself up as reigning queen. That had been her goal since Sina had retired some years ago.

There had been some talk about Kendra not wanting to take the job. Sonya had actually told others that Kendra wasn't fit for the job. It was a rumor that had taken a life of its own when she'd started it, but it fizzled out sooner than she had wanted. But Kendra had proven her rumors to be true over and over. What kind of queen would let her sister marry a mortal, then on top of that, get herself kidnapped? The Lanning family had been a stick in her ass for too long now, and she wanted them dead. But first she had to take the castle.

"My lady?" Sonya looked at the man standing next to her and smiled at him. He'd been her lover the last few nights and it was beginning to show on him. Sonya had certain tastes, and he'd been more than enough for her. But she was thinking he wouldn't stand another night with her. Besides, his wife was making too much ruckus and that just would not do. Sonya had thought about killing her but didn't have time for that right now. She had to save her magic for the coming war. "My lady, the second queen is wishing a word with you."

"Sina?" He nodded. "Tell her to fuck off. Better yet, tell her I said to roll herself up on a pile of crap and die. It would do the world a big service if she did."

"I cannot say that to...she would have me beheaded should I say...I cannot say that to the second queen." She didn't think he would, but she wouldn't have such problems. But not today. "When should I tell her that you will meet her?"

"I'm not. Going to meet her today or any other day. Not on her terms anyway. I'll see her when I see her and not before." She'd heard someone say that in a movie and she'd never gotten to use it before. Sonya thought it was funny when the man in front of her only stared at her, shocked. "Just ignore her. If she asks again, tell her that I didn't answer you. Which I didn't. I don't have time to go to tea parties with her today. I have to get this thing moving in the right direction, and I can't keep an eye on things with her breathing down my back."

As he moved away, she thought of the meeting that she had planned with the people in the castle, the war of all wars that was going to make her queen of it all. But there was something worrisome that she'd had to deal with, and right now all she could think about was her helper and where he'd gone. What the hell had happened to her Toby? And then there were the others that she'd hidden in the big building, spies to bring her information and details about the daily goings on of the rest of the family. *Where are they?* she wondered.

Sonya supposed when it came down to it, it didn't matter. Her magic was much stronger, and once she had the power of the ones beside her, nothing would be able to stop her. Glancing to her left, she smiled at the guillotine that she'd had built last week.

The only way to kill one of them was to remove their head. Everyone knew that, but few knew that it had to be done with a silver blade that had been forged in the castle's own smithy house. And fewer still knew that in order to take over the kingdom once they were dead, you had to spill first blood. Something she was going to do as soon as she had them in her clutches.

All she was going to do was nick the queen or the queen mother, and the rest would fall into place. Her magic was going to hold them for her, of course, while she took her silver blade that had been stolen from the smithy himself and cut her deeply enough that blood flowed freely. Then she would bring them here and line them up to have their heads removed. The Lannings, too, would have their heads fall into her woven basket, one that she'd made decades ago when she'd started her plan.

Sonya made her way back to her home. It wasn't her first home, the one she'd grown up in and the one that she had lived in until recently. That house was being watched. Guards were waiting for her to come there so they might arrest her. They thought her a fool was all she could think of, and she had simply never returned.

But there were other things afoot, and she'd yet to figure out who had told the queen where she lived in the first place. Toby had more than likely done it. He'd been so full of himself lately that she'd bet that in a fit of power, he'd mentioned it. No matter, she'd already taken precautions to get to a better location, and this place nearly had everything she wanted in a home. Not her Toby, of course, but if he had told where they lived, she would have killed him anyway. Betrayal was something she did not tolerate.

This house was bigger than her first home, and it had plenty of room for her to plan in. One of the larger rooms on the lower floor had made a perfect office for her, and the room on the upper level had worked out for her play room. A room she used often, for it relaxed her to no end when she was hurting someone softer than her. And she had to admit, everyone was softer than she was. It was the way she loved it.

It had taken some doing to get all her equipment bought and put into this house, but now that she had it all set up, she'd been having so much fun in there she hadn't wanted to leave it. And the men were very willing to do anything she said for them to do when she showed them what she had. Some, sadly, didn't care for the way she had things set up, but she brought them around if she had to.

There had been a few that had told her no. Of course, they'd never lived to talk about her place. Only the select few, the ones that had seemed excited, had been able to continue breathing. She knew that they thought she was going to let them tie her to the iron cross and that they would be the one that would get to use the strap and whips she had there when they were shown to her room. But they figured it out soon enough when they entered, as there was nowhere for them to go until she was done with them. And only a few had made it past the first night. Toby had been one, and this man, Rogers, had been the other. Excited, she made her way up the stairs, turning off the lights as she went.

Blood had been spilled quite a bit in her play room. And as she could not trust any of the people who might act as a servant for her, she'd had to clean things herself. But last night had been a very good night and when she'd finished with Rogers, she'd been just too tired to go back and clean up. Perhaps she'd have him do it tonight.

"And then I'm going to have to find a replacement for him." She didn't want to have to go trolling again. She'd thought of taking a few of the humans to her lair, but they were too soft, puny when it came to the way she liked things, and hadn't been much fun. The screaming and the begging could and did get on her nerves very quickly when they never stopped.

Using a bit of her magic, she locked up the house and then made her way to her planning room. There was still much to do and no time for mistakes. Things had to go fast and had to be done with precision. If not, everything would fail. And Sonya had been planning this for too long for things to go wrong now. It was going to be all hers.

Killing Curtis and Dottie had been something she'd not planned on either. They'd both been close to dying anyway, thanks mostly to them disobeying her and Sonya having to take away her magic. But she knew that Dottie had talked to one of the people from the castle. And no matter what she'd done to her while at the hospital, she would not tell her a name. Killing her had been tricky, but it had to be done. And to make matters worse, someone had blocked Dottie's mind from her and Sonya couldn't even get into her head to see who it was. But they'd both paid, and now that part of this was over. If Dottie had just kept Charleston away from the Lannings, killing them wouldn't have been necessary. But with Charleston and Phillip meeting and the fucking pretend queen finding out, it had brought other things to light.

She'd been messing in the lives of those leopards for their entire lives, and no one had known about it until that damned woman Dottie had let Charlie meet and fall in love with the youngest of them. Damn it all to hell. Their power was going to be hard to deal with. Not impossible, but hard. And it was all Dottie's fault.

The Lanning men had their mates. No matter that she'd taken the first stumbling block in her way out, they'd still managed to meet and fall in love with them. Mates were bad news. Especially when Linyah had been the one she'd been working to get out of the picture in the first place. And now, Sonya was pretty sure their magic had been shared with all of them. Including the women and any children that might be born of them.

"Why must everything be such a problem? When will people learn that my way is the way things are to go?" Sonya giggled. "Oh yeah, when I'm queen they'll know better than to go against me."

It was well after darkness had fallen before she moved out of her room to the main levels of her home. She was surprised to find the house cold and empty, and when she tried to reach for Rogers to ask him where he was, she met with nothingness. She decided that she'd had enough of people treating her as if she were nothing and reached for the door just as someone knocked on it.

Opening it, she was ready to blast the person on the other side for startling her, but she paused when she saw who it was. Manfred wasn't one to come to her home, not even during the day. And the fact that he was covered in blood made her think things were going to be delayed more than she'd thought.

"My lady, there's been an accident." She was right. One of the idiots had done something that was going to make it more difficult to get the royal family to bow before her. "I'm afeared that Rogers has been killed."

When he didn't say anything else, she started tapping her foot. And when that didn't work, she finally spoke. "Well? Was the rest of the work finished up before you left to take care of him?"

"My lady? It was Rogers, he worked for you. He was killed today by a falling tree. We were making more of the arrows that you—"

"And did you finish them? Come, come now. It's not that difficult a question. Did you finish what I assigned you before you came here? Why am I assuming you didn't?" Manfred started stammering about death and Rogers again, but all she could see was more delays and how there simply wasn't time for them. "Tomorrow you will need to start early for work. I need those arrows done now so that I may cover them in magic. That sort of thing does not just happen, you know. And no lunch either, unless you are willing to eat while working. We have less than a day to get ready for this, and I will not tolerate any more delays. Do I make myself perfectly clear?"

As soon as he nodded, she slammed the door in his face. There would be no one to play with tonight, thanks to Rogers's insensitivity. The nerve of the man getting himself killed at this late hour. Didn't he know she was under enough pressure and didn't need him to be doing this to her?

As she made her way up the stairs to her bedroom, she thought of all the things he'd messed up by getting killed.

She would have to go in earlier tomorrow just to make sure that everyone knew the importance of what they were up against. She had been telling them this daily, hourly as the time grew nearer, but apparently they'd forgotten. The thought of taking her whip with her tomorrow and using it on a few of the workers was tempting, but she didn't want to come across as a horrible queen from the start. Sonya thought she'd have to think of other ways to get them motivated again. Then she was going to go and talk to Leila. It was well past the time to do it, and as much as she hated the woman, she had an army that would look good surrounding her when she went up against the castle.

She and Leila, the old Doran queen of her people, had never gotten along. But she knew the woman didn't like the current queen and her family any more than Sonya did. In fact, Sonya had been working on souring that relationship for a great many years, hoping that someday she'd have a use for the old bat. And now that day had come. Tomorrow she was going to go and tell her what she was going to do and, if she was willing, let her be a part of it when they quite literally stormed the castle.

~~~

Leila was nearly ready to go to see her grandson when Durk came to the door. He was smiling an odd smile, and she couldn't help but smile back at him. There was devilment up his sleeve, and she was going to enjoy this.

"Your grandson is here. Alone, should you like to know. He said it is with great urgency that he needs to talk to you very soon. As in the next five minutes, he said." She asked him why that was funny. "Because, my lady, he has brought you a gift."

"A gift? Am I going to like this gift from him?" Durk told her he didn't think so. "Then why, pray tell, are you laughing?"

Something small and fast moved by her butler and into her room. It was a puppy. And when he started barking at her, at a very loud pitch, she snapped her fingers and told him to sit. As soon as he tried, several times as it turned out, his feet slipping out from under his ample butt all the while, she finally bent and picked him up.

That seemed to let him think it was all right to lick every part of her face. Putting her hand over his mouth, she looked him in the eye and told him in no uncertain terms that he wasn't to do that. Max came into the room just as she started to ask Durk to get rid of the thing.

"You like him?" Leila looked at the pup now sitting all over her feet, then at her grandson. "Dad said I should have asked you first, but I thought for sure if you saw him, you couldn't say no. I have his brother at home."

"You got me a dog." Max nodded and kissed her on the doggy wet cheek. "Why would you think a dog would be a good gift? You do know that I am the head of our clan and that I have duties to perform? And a dog, in this case a puppy, is going to require more work than I wish to put into it."

"But when you're here alone and I'm not here, he can keep you company. Look at him, he already knows that you're his master. Now you have to pick a name for him." Several came to mind, but he only looked at her. "You have to give him a name that you can call out in public."

"I see." She sat down and the puppy, worn out from tasting her no doubt, whimpered a little, then rolled to his side and promptly fell asleep. "This isn't the only reason you came here, is it? To disrupt my busy morning by bothering me with a mongrel?"

Max grinned at her. She loved this boy more than she'd ever thought possible, and he had her wrapped tightly around his little finger. He knew as well as she did that she'd drop everything to see him and to spend time with the little monster. And she also knew, as he did, that the puppy would stay with her forever.

"You're going to have company." She knew this, of course, and had been trying to think of a way to avoid her since yesterday. "You have to see her. And if you'd like to do me a big favor, I'd like for you to agree with everything she asks of you."

"You mean this plot of hers to take over the castle." Max nodded and leaned back on the sofa. Leila nodded at Durk when he brought them both tea and cookies, and even a snack for the sleeping dog. "You do know that she's planning to ask me to stand behind her. And to have our kind there with us when she goes before the queen."

"I do. And bring all the men and women that you can gather." She asked him what he was planning. "Nothing really. I mean, I'd like for you to be there with her to keep her from running should she try. And your men there will be able to subdue the others should they try and be brave. I don't think they will. Once Sonya is taken, I think they'll simply lay down their arms and give up."

"But you're not sure." He shook his head. "Do you know what she's planning to do there? I mean, besides try and take the castle?"

"Some. It's like some of its easy to see and some of it's murky and cloudy. I tried to concentrate harder, but all I got for my troubles was a headache and a bloody nose." She worried that he couldn't see it all. Max was stronger than she was, and he wasn't even a full-blooded Doran. She wondered what children of his would be able to do. "Grandma, do you suppose it's murky because it can change?"

"That could be it. Or it could be something that you're not to see. Something that happens that you are a part of. I have taught you the rules of seeing in the future. You know that you cannot change what is yours or the ones you love." He nodded at her, but she could see that he was distressed about it. "Let me talk to this witch today and see what I can find out from her. Perhaps she's changing the game on us and we'll have to wait for her."

"All right." But he didn't seem to think it was finished, so she sipped her tea and ate two cookies before he spoke again. "Mom is going to have a baby."

Leila knew that. All the women, it seemed, were breeding in the Lanning family but one. And she'd be that way soon enough too. But to look at her grandson, she thought it was more than that. Much more.

"You're going to have a sister or brother, I guess. And I'll be a grandmother again. I'm looking forward to that, aren't you?" He grinned and said he wasn't going to be a grandmother at all. "Very funny. What has you upset? The baby or the fact that you think they'll pick it over you?"

"No. Carter said he'd never do that. And I believe him. Nah, it's not that. Mom will be a great mom." Leila waited. "She took the job as sheriff the other day. I mean, she needed to do it. It'll keep her closer to home."

Whatever was bothering Max, it had to do with this new job. She started to ask him, but Durk interrupted her. He said that Miss Sonya was here and she would like a meeting. Leila looked at Max when he stood up.

"Tell me what it is." He shook his head. "A favor for a favor. You tell me and I'll do this for you. You know I would have anyway, but I'll look, and you know that will cause me great harm."

"She has to kill someone." Leila nodded. She knew that her daughter had been a cop, and a damned good one too. And she thought perhaps she'd killed before. "Not like this. Not this time. She has to kill them because of me."

"How so?" He pulled free of her and started pacing. "Max, you know your mother would give her life for you. For any of your new family too. But like you, she's an immortal. Nothing will happen to either of you."

"This man comes for me. He tries to get me to do things for him. Not sexual, but for him. I get myself caught. And no matter how many times I try to look, I can't figure out what I did to get there. But he takes me and…and Dad gets hurt. Then Mom has to shoot someone she knows. Someone that she loves."

Durk came to the door again, but he only stood there. That damned woman was here and as much as she wanted to kick her out on her ass, Max had asked her to help him. Standing up, she pulled him into her arms and held him. It was then she realized how tall he'd gotten. He looked up at her when she said his name softly.

"Don't let this worry you too much, all right?" He nodded. "Your mother loves the Lanning family and all it entails, correct? She's never let anyone hurt any of you, no matter what."

"I know that. They're our family. She said that we were very lucky to have them in our lives." Leila nodded. So was she. "You're going to tell me it can't be one of them, aren't you?"

"Sort of. But what if it was one of them? What if it was Carter or one of the others that she had to shoot just to get them out of harm's way, or you out of it? What if it was the only way to save you?" He just stared at her. "Max, think about what you said. You said she has to shoot someone. Not behead them. Not take a sword and remove their body parts one at a time until they were in pieces, but to shoot them. Ghastly as it all sounds, you can't be killed by a bullet."

"It won't kill them." He let out a long harsh breath before he continued, as if hearing her say it somehow confirmed it for him. "It might hurt them pretty badly, but it won't kill them. They'll be safe."

"Yes. And so will you." He nodded, and she could see that he felt a great deal better about it. So did she, as a matter of fact. "So, back to this sorcerer. Are you sticking around or are you going to leave me with her? All alone. In my house."

Max laughed. "I think you can handle her. And as much as I'd like for you to just kill her and be done with it, I think this needs to happen." She asked him why. "So that in the future, no one else will get it in their head to do something against the queen."

Making an example of her sounded good to Leila. Then perhaps things would settle around here. It was getting almost to the point where she wanted to move in with her daughter and new son just to keep them safe at all times with her magic. Not yet, but it was getting there. Smiling, she walked to the door with Max and then stared at Durk. She asked him if he'd taken in refreshments.

"No, my lady." He grinned. "If I should, I would suggest that you don't partake. It might make you wish you hadn't."

"Why, you sly devil you. When did you get so sneaky?" He grinned bigger at her. "Ah, you've been that way all along and I've only just noticed."

"Correct, my lady. Your…guest, she is waiting. And I should like to tell you something more." She asked him what. "Do not give her your back."

She thought that an excellent idea and told him so. As soon as she entered the big room where Sonya had been seated, she felt as if she'd been put with an imposter. The woman practically oozed good will and charm. She was buttering her up for the kill, as Max would have said, and Leila let her fawn all over her, agreeing with what she needed, even going so far as to suggest that her men come too. It was over, this plan of Sonya's, almost before it began as far as Leila was concerned. Yes, this was going to be fun, she thought. And she had a front row seat to it all.

CHAPTER 11

Phillip felt amazing. He stretched out and reached for his cock when it felt warm and curled his hand in her hair. When he opened his eyes and looked down at the beauty that was sucking his cock, all he could think about was he could wake this way every morning and never tire of it.

"Come up here. I want to enjoy you too." She shook her head and cupped his balls tightly in her hand. "I want to come inside of you then. Ride me."

When Charlie lifted her head from him, he moaned. Christ, she was gorgeous right now, and he wanted to throw her back on the bed and pound her. As he reached for her, she shook her head and backed away.

"I want to taste you coming down my throat." Phillip nodded, not sure he could have spoken anything that would have made sense anyway. "When you do, I'm going to get you hard again. Then I'm going to let you fuck me, all day, until I can't move."

"I love that plan." He watched her lower her head to him once again and cried out when instead of taking him into her mouth, she licked him from root to tip then circled his crown. "Please, baby, you're going to kill me."

When she swallowed around him, her throat muscles tightening around him, Phillip rocked his hips upward until she did it again. Fucking her this way, feeling her hands on his body, made him cry out every time she gave his balls another squeeze. And when she fisted him, her mouth open to catch his cum, Phillip watched as his release shot from his cock to her face as she finished him off this way. But he was far from done with the beauty.

He needed more, and was pretty sure that she did as well. When he jerked her up to him and rolled her to her back, he slammed his cock deep even before she wrapped her legs around him. Phillip fucked her as hard as he could, pounding her even as he heard her scream out her first, then second and third release before he emptied in her once again. As he dropped over her, he heard her soft giggle when he rolled to his back, taking her with him.

"You were supposed to let me do the work. Why must you take over every time?" He laughed with her. "I would like, one time, to have my way with you. Do you think you can manage that?"

Not even thinking about it, he told her no. "You are far too sexy and much too gorgeous for me to simply lay still while you have your fun. Do you have any idea how much I love making you come, hearing you scream out my name when you've peaked? Christ, it's all I can do to remember to breathe when I'm inside of you, much less let you be in charge."

"I love you." He held her closer to him as he told her he loved her as well. "I have so much to do today, I thought I'd start our day off right before we had to leave here."

"You can do this every day, and I'm pretty sure it will make anything better for me. But I'm sorry about working today. Misha told us yesterday that we had to go in and finish up some paperwork. I know that I've been leaving you alone a lot, but it's my job." She lifted her head up and looked at him. "Christ, I really do love you."

"And I love you. But...I do have a job too. Not much of one just yet, but I'm working on it." He knew that she was bored and had wondered if she was going to try and find a place to work on her baskets again. He remembered the buildings downtown.

"Hey, we own a building. Well, four of them actually, and you should go down and see what can work for you." She had been in the process of standing up and turned to him when he spoke. "I won't be able to tell you if you don't find something to cover with. I am a much neglected man."

"You are a very strange man is what you are. What are you talking about? What buildings do we own?" She pulled on her robe, much to his disappointment, but he could think better. When she asked him again, he smiled.

"The county seat is trying to generate businesses downtown by selling off some of the older but in good shape buildings along Main Street and a few of the side ones. Much like revamping, I guess. Max told me about it. Anyway, I did him a solid by putting in a bid for the one he wanted, and bought four of them for my own use. Misha did as well, but I don't know how many he got. For all I know—" She cleared her throat. He had to think where he'd been going with his story when he remembered. "But we own four of them. You should go and have a look at them and take one for your own business. I'm going to have to put someone in them in the next sixty days before the first payment is due, so one of them might as well be you. That way you don't have to worry about getting a barn put here."

"How big are they?" He said that one was a warehouse, but the others were just businesses that had gone under at some point. "And I can just move into one of them. No problem."

"I think it might need some work, like to be cleaned up and stuff. They've been closed up for some time. One I know for sure has been for at least ten years, the other maybe longer than that. But I've been assured that they're structurally sound and that all the wiring is replaced. I guess about five months ago the town thought about using them for something and had them brought up to code. But other than that, I don't know." He thought of something else. "You know that Carter has this apartment complex, don't you? Well, it's filled with some people, families mostly, that have been down on their luck. Maybe a few of them would be able to help you out. Cleaning up or even working with you."

"I don't know anything about having people working for me."

He nodded and decided to have someone talk to her about it. Giving those people a helping hand as well as some money to spend would help out everyone, and he thought he'd try to make it work for him as well.

When she entered the bathroom, her cell started to ring. He told her, but she said to answer it. Only his family had the number, so it had to be one of them. It was Murph.

"I was going to go into town and wanted to see if Charlie wanted to join us. Your mom and sisters are going with us. Not Linyah. I guess she has to work, but the rest of us are. She said she might come over later. We're going to have some lunch and buy some baby things for Hannah before the shower next month. Oh, and I wanted to say thanks before I forget for helping Max out. He is excited about being a property owner." He told her it had been his pleasure and told her what he done and how he'd had mentioned it to Charlie too. "So you think she'll move into one of them?"

"I don't know. I hope so. It would be nice for her to have her old job back, as well as doing something that she's really good at. I told her about the people that live in Carter's apartment building too, and she's nervous about that. I know little about hiring people, but Carter has done all the background checks and things, so that will be one less thing to worry about too." Murph said she liked that idea as well. "You talk to her. Not into it, but just talk to her. And if she's all right with it, we can have her things moved in when it's ready."

"Did you know that she's still paying rent on her other house? I'm sure that someone is going to have to go there and clean that out as well. I can arrange it, call in a few favors." He said he'd ask Charlie. "Good plan. By the way, you should know that Max might be hanging around with you guys at the office today, and for a few days too. I think he wants something to do between classes. Maybe you guys can have him sweep up or something. I don't know."

He did know. Max was a whiz at a great many things, and could make a computer do just about anything as well. They'd just had their systems updated recently, but he wanted to see if Max wanted to work for other businesses around town. Like Charlie's when she was set up, and other places that might need someone to come in and just get them started. It would make him a few bucks and keep him from being bored.

As soon as Charlie got out of the shower, he told her what was going on. And when he mentioned to her about having someone go and get her other house cleaned out, she agreed with him. It was time, she told him.

"I have some things in storage too. Not a great deal, mostly some baskets that I got really cheaply." He started writing things down as she dressed. "And there is the rental agreement I had with the landowner. I don't know what he'll do about my deposit, but it was a pretty hefty amount."

"I don't think I told you, but...well, we're rich. I mean, what my mom called nasty stinking rich. I'm just putting that out there so you know that if he does take your deposit, it won't be that bad for us." She sat down on the chair with her blouse half buttoned. "We had money, all of us did, before we met our mates. I mean, billions. Rider had the most by then, but.... Anyway, after Linyah and Thomas married, we sort of, as a family, got more."

"How much more?" Her voice was low and sort of scary, but he sat down to answer her. So he told her, ball park. "No, seriously."

"Actually, there's more than that, but...I don't know how much. At one time Nildale said he didn't think there was a number for the amount of money we were to get as family, so we sort of rounded it to something that we knew." He watched her face. It was a good face and one that he would love dearly for the rest of their days together. "I have invested well and done some things with—"

When she raised her hand up, he stopped talking. It was funny really, the way she seemed to be in a state that he thought of as comatose. But when she got up to move back and forth in front of him, he not only watched her face but her lovely ass too. She caught him looking at the latter of the two.

"I'm being serious here and you're thinking of my ass." Nodding, he grinned at her. "This...why didn't you...why would you not...?"

"Why would I not what?" She told him. "I didn't tell you before because it never came up. I mean, I should have, sure, but I simply never thought of it. We have money and that's all I really cared about. And I have you that makes it all worthwhile."

"And these buildings you bought. You think to turn them into more money, don't you? I mean, you can never have too much, right?" He wasn't sure what she was getting at, but the anger was there so he asked her what she meant by that. "You want it all. All the money in the world."

"No. I don't. I didn't ask for what I got. So having more...are you pissed because we have money or is there—?"

"*We* don't have money. You do." Phillip started to laugh, but he could see that she was serious, and he stood up to go to her. "Don't touch me right now. I'm sort of angry."

"No, you're not. You're upset, but not angry. I'm sorry I didn't tell you sooner. I honestly never thought about it." Charlie nodded. "If it makes you feel any better, I would give it all back if that's what it takes."

"You most certainly will not." He laughed when she did. "I'm sorry. I've been struggling to get my business off the ground for years before it finally paid off. Then when the money started to come in, this stupid thing with the book started. Then the tumor, and now this dumb woman that wants to take over the kingdom."

"Yeah, we have to deal with her tomorrow, did you know that?" She nodded and told him that Murph had told her. "Good. And when we get there, we're going to have to stand together. Did she tell you that?"

"Yes. Do you think this woman will get what she wants?" He told her there wasn't any way for her to win against all of them. "And this thing with us, you think that she'll convince someone that you and I aren't supposed to be together? And they'll pull us apart?"

"No. Never." The doorbell sounded throughout the house, and he knew it was Murph and the other women. "You go and have a good time. See the buildings with the others and pick which one will best suit your needs. Then we'll think of something to do with the other three."

After she was gone, he and Rocco worked out a schedule to have someone come in and do some of the repairs on the house. There wasn't much to be done, but enough that it would require more time than he had to devote to it. When it was settled that Rocco would take care of it all, Phillip left the house knowing that it would be taken care of. Just as he was leaving, however, Misha pulled into the drive to give him a lift to work. It was out of the ordinary, but he got in his car with him just to see what was up. Because he knew there was something.

"I have a favor to ask." Phillip said that he'd do it. "You don't even know what it is. For all you know, I could be asking you to cut off your dick. I'm not, but don't say that unless you mean it."

"I do." Misha looked at him before looking at the road again. When he didn't say anything, Phillip decided to fill the quiet with what he was up to. "Charlie is going to go and look at those buildings with the women today. And I'm supposed to warn you that Max is coming by as well."

Phillip knew that he wasn't paying any attention to him when he nodded. There was something wrong, but he'd never pry. Not unless it became necessary. But when they pulled in the lot of their business, neither of them made any attempt to get out.

"I don't want to do this anymore." Phillip said nothing. He was sort of shocked, but waited for Misha to explain. "I mean, I really loved it for a long time, but now...now I find myself wanting to hurry through the work to get back home and be a husband and father. It's not...it was never fun, but I'm simply worn out by all the devastation."

"Carter is still having a hard time too. I mean, not as bad since he met Murph, but he's still has bad days." Misha nodded. "So what was the favor you needed from me?"

"It's not really a favor so much as...what do you think of this? I mean, is this something you can see yourself doing forever?" Phillip wanted to tell him he hated it, but that really wasn't it either. He just, like his brother, had had enough.

He told him he didn't much care for it any more either. "It's all bad news. I mean we can make a difference, and we do, but nothing is ever just a happy ending. There is always tragedy. I'm all for just not going to work either. I'm...I'm seriously over it all, Misha."

Misha nodded but stared out the window before he spoke. Phillip had a feeling it was because he was trying hard not to be excited about closing up shop.

"We have money. More than we can spend. But that was never it. It's that, like you said, we made a difference. But there is only so much a person, a family, can take that is all bad news."

Phillip agreed with him by nodding his head. "What is it you want to do, Misha? Have you talked to the rest of them?" He said that he'd not, that he just wanted to talk to him. "And what do you think they'll say? Rider has been bitching for some time now that we're not doing anything that the locals couldn't be doing. Andrew just said the other day he wanted to take a vacation, and we got five calls in a row right after. Thomas is gone more than he is here. Carter wants to work with Murph at the police station, and I want to have a family. One that I can be there for all the time. Hell, I think I might even enjoy being a stay at home dad."

"I've been thinking that too. Hannah has it in her head that she wants to work with your wife when she opens her place up. Mom has really been having so much fun with her gardening clubs and those book of the month things. She doesn't work for us much anymore, but I think she'd be thrilled not to have to fill in either." Misha laid his head back against the seat and closed his eyes before continuing. "I have to tell you, Phillip, I feel better already about this. Knowing that someone feels the same as I do about shutting down."

"Good. When?" Misha laughed, and said they should talk to the others first. "Yeah, so when? I need to get my life in gear. My wife just found out that I have lots of money, and it occurred to me, I have lots of money. I'd like to go someplace on a plane that does not involve me having to dig through mud and mire for once. And I'd like to lay on a fucking beach with the water flowing over me and not have to look for bodies that might wash up on the shore. I want a life. My own life."

"You really want this? I mean, you're not just saying that to make me feel better." He told him he wasn't. He really wanted this too. "Okay, let's go and see how the others take it. And even if they want to try and make it work, I think that I'm done. I can't...I just can't do this anymore."

~~~

The building was much larger than she'd imagined. Actually, she'd had no idea what to think when they pulled up in front of it, but this one was the smallest of the four and it was still five stories tall. Charlie tried not to be overwhelmed by everything that Phillip had told her before she left this morning.

"You'll have plenty of storage space. Did you see the bigger building out back?" She turned to tell Maribel that she wasn't helping her, but the woman winked. "I was kidding. There are bay areas for unloading, but no more buildings. And on the second floor, I'm to understand there is quite a large open space that has long tables in it. Everything in the building stays, by the way."

"What am I going to do with all this space?" Maribel told her to fill it with lovely things. "But that would be so…do you have any idea how many little bars of soap I can store here? Millions upon millions. I would never use them all. They'd go…why are you nodding your head?"

"You do know that you're going to do much better here than at the other home, right? I mean, you can hire a great many people to come in and help fill the orders. Someone to take the orders, as well as someone to take them away when you're finished with them. Also, there is a great deal of space on this floor where you can sell your leftovers as well as a few things that you might not be able to put into a basket. And I want to work here too. So does Hannah. We want to do this too." Charlie thought of the beautiful blanket that Ruby Luna had given her and asked Maribel why she wanted to work for her. "Why? Well, we're hoping for some discounts, and we want to be with you. It's going to be fun. And Murph is nearly across the street. We can have lunch together all the time."

"And I can pop in when I want to and bring my mom and sister." Charlie nodded at Linyah who had just *popped* in earlier. "Mom said that she'd use your business for all her functions, and there are a great many of them."

"I'm just a small business owner. I'm not equipped to handle large functions." Linyah just patted her on the back as she made her way to the stairs. Charlie looked at Hannah, who was smiling from ear to ear. "This place is simply too big. I mean, he could put anything in here other than just my little business."

"He might, but he sees potential in you and he loves you. Besides, I think you're thinking much too small. You need to think on the grander scale of things." Charlie heard her name and went up the stairs to see what Linyah and Murph had found. She knew that the other two were right behind her.

They'd climbed to the topmost floor, and she could see all of the city from any window. The windows weren't broken this high up. The big desk that sat in the middle of the room was covered in dust and grime, and there was enough dirt on the floor alone that she was sure she could fill a large pit with it. When Murph bent and lifted a corner of what had been a rug, she could see the hardwood floors beneath that looked to be as old as the building. Rubbing her hand over the desk top, she could see that it was made of oak and maybe cherry. She looked at the women in the room, and felt for the first time in a very long time that she was a part of something.

"This is...I have no idea what to say to you guys. 'I love you' seems so weak." When Hannah started crying, she did as well. "I'm sorry. But...with you guys, I feel like I can do this. More than do this, I think I can make it work."

"Of course you can. And we're going to help you." Maribel looked around the room before continuing. "After we get this place cleaned up. I know a wonderful group of women who are just starting out as a cleaning crew. I think it will take more than them, but they can get a start. And someone to come in and fix the windows. I know just the firm for that too."

As Maribel walked to the other side of the room, Charlie looked at Murph. "She's going to take over, isn't she?"

"Nah, but she will have this place spotless in less time than you or I could. She has a knack for getting things done." Murph sat on the desk, unmindful of her clothing. "There's some things that Phillip asked me to talk to you about. The people living in Carter's house could use a hand up."

"I think that's an excellent idea. But I want you to help me out with that. I want some background checks done on them. I know that right now I'm thinking small, but there might be a point where I'm making some good money, and I don't want anyone here that I don't trust." Murph said she would do that, and told her that Carter had already done the checks. "Also...I know this is a lot, but I have a house with my things in it. Not a lot...the place was mostly furnished when I rented it, but the barn things are mine. I'll need help getting it boxed up and brought here. I'll also need a storage unit until this place is usable."

"I can do that." Murph stood up. "You'll need a new name. Grant Me Anything won't work now. And more supplies. I can hook you up with that too."

"You'll be my partner." Murph started to shake her head. "Yes. All of you will be. If we're partners, we'll work together for a common goal rather than all of us going in different directions to help me. Partners, or I say no to this place and doing the business."

"All right." Murph put out her hand, and before Charlie could take it, she spoke again. "So you know, touching me will give you a part of me. I don't know how much, as you seem to have a lot now. But you're going to get something."

"Right now, your friendship is more than enough." As soon as their hands touched, Charlie knew what she'd meant. It was like touching a live wire with wet feet, and she was pretty sure they both felt it.

CHAPTER 12

The morning of the Great War, as Sonya had dubbed it, dawned beautiful and warm. Sonya thought it was a good omen. The flowers in the field where she was meeting Leila were full of tiny buds; the birds, gone quiet now, were still perched in their trees, waiting and watching for something to happen after having their morning disturbed. She looked at her few men and smiled. They were going to win this war and she'd be queen, as she should have been. When Leila showed up, Sonya asked her how she felt about this.

"How do I feel? I think this is a foolish thing that you're doing. I have no idea why anyone...what were you thinking, Sonya, or were you? I mean, really. Why are you doing this? I mean now? Why are you doing this now?" Sonya asked her what she meant. "You have been around as long as I have, Sonya. So I know that you've not just started this planning to do this. Why right now?"

"I have always felt that I should have been queen when Sina retired and they put that upstart of a woman in my place. She has no right to sit upon the throne any more than you do. She is unmated as well as emotional. Why, did you not hear that she'd allowed herself to be kidnapped? That humans had to come and save her? What sort of queen does that?" Leila pointed out that she was the daughter to Sina, a queen of all queens still. "And that should make her a queen? No. She's just too stupid to be queen, while I'm very brilliant."

"Ah." Sonya wasn't sure what that meant but didn't comment. She needed Leila and her army of men. She looked back at them lined up in tight lines and their armor. There were hundreds of them. "What is the plan? I'm assuming that we're not going to stand here until they simply come out and give themselves up, are we?"

That was what Sonya had planned. To her way of thinking, once they saw what a great army they had, the queen would come sobbing out of the castle and simply beg for her life. She was slightly embarrassed that she had nothing more to offer the Doran.

"I'm going to storm the castle." But that was going to be hard. First of all, it was still miles from them, and in order to walk that far...it would take the wind out of her army. They had magic, not fighting skills.

"I think you should have thought this through better. Why don't we all go home and we can do this when you're more organized?" Sonya felt her temper snap, but before she could do or say anything, Leila spoke again. "Do it and I'll end your very life right here. I've no time for foolishness."

A great white horse could be seen coming toward them. It was a winged one, she could see now, a Pegasus. *Oh, to have gotten a few of them,* Sonya thought just as the rider and horse landed with a soft thud before them. It was Kendra, the queen, and before she could dismount, the rest of the royals were there too. Even the Lannings were there, their huge leopards just suddenly appearing.

Sonya had a sudden thought. This was a bad idea. A fucking horrifically bad idea. And she was afraid it was too late to do anything about it. As the former king and queen stood with the cats, Kendra walked toward her and Leila. Before she could do more than think about lifting up her sword, she was disarmed and lifted several inches from the ground. Magic held her as tightly as her belt did around her waist even as Kendra's fingers dug deep in her throat. The only difference was her belt wouldn't kill her. This woman, in all her fury, could and would.

"I should simply end you now and be done with your ass." Sonya swallowed twice before she found her tongue. But Kendra spoke again. "What did you hope to gain by this display? You were never going to take my castle. And you know as well as I do the rules of magic. Just what do you think you're going to be able to do now that you're here?"

"I have an army." Kendra looked behind her, and Sonya knew that she could see them all. "I will win against you. You are lazy and without the army that I lead. Put me down and I'll make your death quick." Sonya had no intentions of making her death anything but long and painful, but the queen had no way of knowing that.

"Oh really? And just how did you plan to accomplish this, Sonya? Making my death, slow or quick, would be impossible for you. As for you having your own army, have you seen what I have with me?" Sonya had and started to laugh. "Hold your tongue. I have the great army behind you, the one in front of you, and should you look to my sky, you'll see them there as well."

The shadow fell over her, and she glanced up. It was all she could do with Kendra holding her this way. But she saw them. It was more than enough to tell her that the dragons, long since dormant, had been woken and were now flying over her and her men. Then it occurred to what she'd said about the army behind her.

"That is my army. The one that I brought with.... What do you mean you have them at my back? There are no men at my back that I do not own." Leila cleared her throat and she looked at her. "You said you'd fight with me. That you'd help me take the castle from this upstart. You cannot back away now."

"Actually, all I said was that I'd come here with my people. I never said I'd fight with you. It was never my intention to do more than what my grandson asked me to do. He said to come with you and I have."

Sonya felt her anger soar out of control. Laughter...she could hear it echoing in her head as well as all around her. When she lifted her hand to touch Kendra's arm to jerk free she was thrown back, her body flying far before it hit something solid behind her. The big cat stood before her and growled loudly.

Her body was hurting. The pain of it, and it was everywhere, was making her breathing painful. She couldn't lift her arms. Her fingers even felt like someone had crushed them with a stone. The leopard who had thrown her here never moved, his body at the ready to pounce. His fur, his beautiful fur, stood on end as he showed her his teeth.

Then Kendra was at his side, her fingers dusting gently over his fur. The smile that she gave her told Sonya that she was going to die and there wasn't a thing she could do about it. But she was going to try.

"Take my men as prisoners, but I will serve you."

Kendra turned, and they watched as the eleven men she'd brought with her laid down their arms when told to.

Then as they knelt low with their necks outstretched, their heads were removed by a single blow to each from the army that Leila had brought with her. Sonya looked at Kendra when she spoke.

"You have caused an upheaval against my castle. You brought those men, men who trusted you, to their deaths by them coming here and laying their lives on the line for you. Because of what you did today, because of the way you acted out, you too will be beheaded." Sonya told her that it was unfair, that she deserved better than them. "And why do you think that?"

"Because I am a great woman. Please. I made a mistake." Kendra reached out and touched her finger to her arm. Almost as soon as she realized she'd been healed, Sonya was jerked from the rock wall behind her and thrown to the ground. The man standing over her, clothed all in black, held his sword to his chest, waiting for some sort of sign. "I'm a good person. I just thought I could do a better job than you. I still believe that, but I won't try to kill you anymore. Let me go and I'll even go to the castle now and advise you on matters that I see you lacking in."

"You still do not understand, do you?" Sonya asked her what was to understand. "You are going to die, Sonya. Today, this very hour. Do you have any idea why you're going to be killed? Do you still believe that you can bargain for your life when you were going to give me no such quarter?"

"Yes. But you have it all wrong. Because you think that I'll come back and try this again. I won't. This was doomed for failure from the start. I should have planned better. Had more men. I just thought that with my powerful magic that I could take you and the family. I even researched how to do it. Beheading royalty is not as simple as it looks." When

Kendra laughed, Sonya looked up at her with a smile. "You like that I have done some work on this?"

"No. I don't really care, but if you thought your magic would work against me and my family, you should have done more research. You know the rules with magic as well as anyone, Sonya. You cannot use it against another person without causing great harm to yourself." Sonya asked her what she meant. "Go ahead and use your considerable power against me. I will allow you one time to show the world here just what happens to magic in my kingdom. Or anywhere for that matter. It's the way of the land."

Sonya felt empowered. Standing up with the help of the man who would have beheaded her, she tried to think of her strongest spell. This was going to be great. Her mind kept rolling around the fact that Kendra was so stupid that she'd let her, Sonya, take her down. When the magic came to her, she nodded once and looked at the upstart.

The power tingled along her arms, and her body felt gifted, stronger than it ever had. When she decided that killing the woman would be her best bet, Sonya unleashed her magic and shoved it as hard as she could at Kendra.

Nothing seemed to be happening. And when Kendra took a step toward her, Sonya thought that she'd lied to her. It shouldn't have surprised her, but she was pissed. Then the burning in her arms began.

"You see, you can't use your magic on us. None of the family, and most certainly against those that have done nothing to you. It comes back on you tenfold. In your research, did you come across that?" She had, but never thought it applied to what she was doing. It was for a greater cause. Her being queen would negate that little rule. Sonya felt the earth move under her feet when she realized what Kendra was saying was true. "You feel it, don't you,

Sonya? The magic, the power of it. Imagine what it was that
you so carelessly tried to use on me. Now multiply it times
ten, then ten, then ten again. You'll see that you never had a
chance to harm any of us. Even had you gotten into the
castle, you would have been powerless against us."

"Make it stop." All of her insides were burning. Not
just her skin now, but her stomach, her muscles, as well as
her brain. "Please, it hurts."

The muscles in her legs could no longer hold her up,
and Sonya fell to the ground. As she watched, looking at
her bare feet, she could see them shrivel, the burning skin
falling off in great pieces. Bones that had been burned dry
broke and blew away in the slight wind. On her hands, too,
each finger dropped off, falling into her lap and burning
hotly through her dress. She was burning from the inside
out, and the pain was excruciating.

"I will not help you, Sonya. To do so would make me
seem weak. And wasn't that one of the things you told
everyone I was? I must show that I'm a good leader so that
no one will try this again. You will be an example to them
all."

Kendra started away just as Sonya felt her head
explode in pain. Before her vision was gone, she saw the
great leopard coming toward her, his huge head just at her
face.

"Kill me." He didn't, of course, and she suffered all the
more for him being so close, watching her as if she were a
grand play on the stage. Just as the pain took her under,
Sonya wondered what she'd been thinking. Better planning
would have kept her alive.

~~~

Kendra hadn't moved since she'd come back to the
castle. Nildale was worried for his little girl. This had been

harder on her than anything she'd ever done before. He moved into her private garden and sat on the seat across from her. If she noticed him, she didn't say anything. Several swans walked around the small pond that had been put in for her recently, a gift from her mother and him.

"I need a mate." He didn't know what to say to her statement, so said nothing. When she continued, he knew that she'd been thinking of this for a long time, not just over this day. "I need someone that I can crawl into his arms and let him hold me while I sob out my hurt and pain."

"I would hold you should you allow me to." She looked at him, and he felt his heart break for her. Tears stained her cheeks, and her nose was pink from her sorrow. "She left you no choice, love. You know that, don't you?"

"It doesn't make it any better to deal with. I didn't care for her either, but she was a person, just like us. A nasty one, but a person all the same." Nildale nodded and wiped his handkerchief over his own nose and eyes. "I would ask a favor of you and Mom. It's a big one, so wait before you answer me."

"You know that we'd do anything that you wish. Anything." She nodded and smiled at him. It was painful as a father to watch his child hurt and know that there was nothing at all he could do about it. As she got up to go to the swan now in the water, he kept a careful eye on her. "What is it you wish, child?"

"I would like a vacation. Not here...I've been here for so long that I've...in the other world. Where Linyah and Nic go. There are places I'd like to see. Parks with trees as big as castles. Oceans that have animals in them that are as big a ship. I want to ride a coaster, have sand between my toes. I want to walk along a beach, barefoot and without guards or others scurrying to see what my needs are.

Trying to anticipate them before I say anything." She let out a long breath as she continued. "I'd like to sleep under the stars, eat what Max has called fire foods, a hot dog on a stick burnt over an open flame. I'd like to wear shorts and jeans. T-shirts and flip-floppers. I want to be free of all, of everything, for a time."

"And you wish for us to keep the castle for you." When she turned to him and smiled, Nildale thought he'd do just about anything for her to do that more often. He knew that she'd not been happy for some time. The rift that had been between her sister and her had been recently mended, but he could see that it hadn't been enough. "We can do that for you. I would ask that you do not go alone to these places. You are the queen, and I'd like for you to be safe."

"No. Alone. Or with one of the others to take me. Max said that he'd go with me to some of the places. He wishes to sleep in his back yard. To have a fire to warm him, food should he need it, and to have a tent if the weather proves to be uncooperative. I would like to join him." Nildale was warming to the idea. Max would be a good escort. But the boy, for all his smarts, was still just a twelve-year-old. "And I'd very much like it if no one knew who I was. I will be only Kendra...I've no last name, but I'll think of one. Kendra, who has some money and is having a wonderful time discovering herself."

He wanted to go, too. Not with her, of course, but to have fun as she was telling him. But he'd do this for her. Not because she'd asked him to, but because she needed it. And badly, he thought. Then he remembered what she'd said when he'd first come out here.

"And a male? Do you suppose to find him while you are discovering yourself?" She said that she didn't know and really only wanted to go and have fun for a time. "All right then. But I do think you need a male in your life. As you said, someone that can hold you like none other."

"Dad, you and Mom have a wonderful relationship. Even Linyah is happy as I've ever seen her, but for me...I just don't think it's going to happen for me. I'm a queen and any male that I find would have to be able to stay in the background, let me run the castle, and few men, hardly any, would be that understanding." He asked her why he'd have to stay in the background. "Because I am queen."

It was the dumbest thing he'd ever heard. It was as if she was saying that any male that she had in her life would be too stupid to stand beside her, to be a helpmate in any way. But she was happy right now, smiling again, and he didn't have it in him to tell her she was wrong. Because in this, he was sure that she was.

As they worked out some of the details of what she was going to do, he reached for his own mate and told her what was going on. He could hear her fear over their daughter being alone in a place they only knew a little of, but she was happy too. And when she came to join them, now in the study, Sina said nothing to their daughter about her plans for a male. Nildale could see, too, that Sina was as happy as he was that Kendra was smiling. But after their daughter left them, he pulled his mate into his arms and held her. When she started to shake, he thought she was crying until she looked up at him.

Tears of laughter were streaming down her face. Her eyes were alight with humor, and he couldn't help it, he smiled as well. When he asked her what was so funny, it took her several starts and stops to tell him.

"Her. When she falls in love. I should like to see her face when she does. I think her male will be...strong, because he will need to be, but he will not take her putting him in his place. I hope that she meets a man that...well, is a great deal like you are. You would never let me put you behind me. Not even when it was good for you." He remembered those days with a lovely sort of fondness and smiled again. "You were such a wonderful king, Nildale. And whoever she finds, he will be as well. We can only hope so."

Nildale had a feeling that he was going to be something else. Something more than his daughter was expecting. Yes, sir, he thought, his daughter was going to be in for a very rude awakening. And he, for one, was looking forward to it.

CHAPTER 13

Charlie was scrubbing the desk when she heard someone behind her. Turning, she knew before she looked who it was, and she smiled at Phillip. He moved toward her, slowly and with purpose. She stood waiting for him.

"Seeing you bent over that desk brings to mind all sorts of things I could be doing to you. I could have you screaming in seconds if you'd let me." Her body heated up, and she could feel her nipples tighten in her bra. "I can smell you. The way your body is calling to mine. I'd like to see just how wet you are."

"There are people just downstairs." He told her that he'd sent them to lunch. "So you could come up here and ravish me."

"Yes." He turned her around and pushed her down on the desk. "I have some news to tell you, but right now I want to fuck you slowly like this."

He pulled her shorts down over her hips, and she felt the coolness of the fan in the room blow over her. Instead of cooling her off, it only served to heat her more. And when Phillip started to rub his hands up and down her ass, she moaned and pressed back against him. She wanted him as much as he did her.

193

"Do you have any idea how beautiful I find this part of you? I find all of you gorgeous, but your ass is nice and firm, and I love holding onto your hips while I take you. My cat wants to take yours this way again. Run you down like he did last night. Fuck his mate hard so that I can have you afterwards." His cat had chased her all over the woods until she was knocked down from behind and ordered to strip. She'd come so many times that she'd been dizzy from it. "He loves the taste of you. The way you come down his throat over and over."

Phillip's cock touched her pussy, and she moaned. Moving back, trying to get him to fill her, he smacked her ass hard and she nearly came from it. He spanked her twice more before he leaned over her and pulled her blouse up and over her head. Her bra was lifted as he cupped her breasts in his hand. His cock, thick and hard, slid between her thighs but never inside of her.

"Phillip, please. I need to come." He told her she would. Soon. "Now. I need to come now. I want to feel you fucking me this way."

His cock slid near her clit again, and she wanted to turn and hit him. He must have known that she was nearly violent with him and pulled back and slammed hard into her. Charlie could have sworn she saw stars when she came, and her entire body seemed to scream at her that it needed more. When he pounded her hard enough to move the desk several feet, she slid her fingers into her pussy and felt Phillips hot wet cock as it filled her over and over.

He nipped at her shoulder, and pulled at her breasts. Dizziness from all the sensations nearly had her closing her eyes, but she wanted to see if stars danced again when she came. Because she knew as surely as she was gearing up for a climax, this one was going to be the best one she'd ever had. And when Phillip sank his teeth into her shoulder, tearing at her flesh, Charlie's breath stopped, and she was sure that her heart did as well. Then it took her.

Even knowing that it was going to be huge hadn't prepared her for her release. She had no breath to scream. Her heart was pounding so hard she was sure that she could have seen it had she been able to look, and every cell in her body seemed to have paused in the moment before to marvel at the feeling. Her climax took everything from her, including her vision.

Waking in Phillip's arms startled her. She looked up at him, his head leaning back on the chair that had only just been delivered that morning. He was sleeping, his body relaxed, his eyes closed. But when she moved, he looked down at her and smiled.

"I thought I'd killed you." She smiled at him, and he smiled back. "That was fantastic. No, that's too tame a word. That was fan-fucking-tastic. Christ, I really…words just fail me on that. Are you all right?"

"Yes. No. I have no idea. What did you do to me?" He told her he had no idea, but he'd love to try and do it again. "Not today. If you tried it again, I think you might just kill me. But my God, that was really amazing."

He held her after that, both of them basking in the afterglow of making love. The desk was no longer where it had been when she'd come up here; they'd managed to move it nearly to the windows. And she thought perhaps she liked it better there. The other things, the boxes of supplies that she would need, letterheads and other items, were in this room, as the storage room had yet to have shelves finished. But for now she was content to have the mess in here.

"I don't have a job." She looked up at him when he continued to stare out the window. "I mean, we're going to finish out the month, but Misha is already making plans to close up the rescue business. He asked me this morning what I thought."

"Will you be all right not doing it any longer?" Charlie knew that Hannah didn't like being alone with Misha gone so much. And even working in the office as she had been, Charlie didn't like it. And Charlie also knew that Carter had been having thoughts of leaving anyway. He'd been plagued with nightmares off and on for some time now.

"Yes. And when Misha asked the others what they thought about it, he and I both were surprised at how badly they wanted out, too. Not that we didn't enjoy it for the most part, but it's not really an easy job. And it does take us away a great deal. Nearly all of us have families now, and we want to be here." Charlie nodded but reached up and pulled Phillip's face to her when he still hadn't looked at her. "I have no idea what to do now."

"You're not without the funds to do whatever you want, you know that right?" He nodded. "So? What do you want to do?"

"I have no idea. I mean, since I was a teenager we've been doing the search and rescue thing. I've never worked at another job. Never flipped burgers or delivered newspapers. The only thing I've done is that."

"Do you want to deliver newspapers? Or work in a restaurant?" He said not really. "Then go out and find a project. You have several empty buildings that you need to work on. There are any number of jobs that need to be finished around the house. You wanted to expand the kitchen pantry. Do it. The pool house needs a new roof…you know, don't do that one. You might fall and break your neck."

"Thanks." He pulled her up on his lap more and she sat across him. He was dressed, as was she, and she figured that he'd done it for both of them. She could also hear the rest of the workers, people from Carter's apartment complex, coming back to work below them. "What if I told you that I'd like to open a hardware store? Not the big kind that is down the road and sells everything from screws to house kits, but one that has the odds and ends in it that are used for antiques. Like leather hinges to order. Odd cut glass. Colored glass that can be used in stain glass replacement."

She liked the idea. "I used to deal with this company that only sold old buttons. I was surprised when I found this out, but after I did, I used them a lot. People like getting old buttons for gifts for some reason. One of my recipients told me that she pours them out on the table and separates them into categories, then makes up a story to go with each one. She's a writer that had a button as her logo. I've read her things — she's pretty racy."

"You're supposed to say 'no, Phillip, get a real job.'" She just stared at him. "That's not what I want you to say, but what you should say. It's what my mom is going to say. After she pops me in the back of the head."

"I fill baskets up with odds and ends for a living. Shop for people with too much money and no time to do it for themselves. I once shopped for a nine-year-old little boy when his father was on his honeymoon with his fourth wife, and was told to spend five grand on his birthday gifts so he could outdo the boy's mother. If anyone needs popped in the back of the head it would be me." She stood up and went to her window near the desk and pulled out a sheet of paper from the top of the desk. "Here, read this."

He took it and read it. "'Black basket filled with every kind of black thing you can find. Even if it's just a can of black paint. Black rocks, a black rose. I want the bitch to know that her heart is black as shit.'" Phillip asked her what it was.

"My first order. I was shocked to say the least, but I filled it. And you know what?" Phillip shook his head. "She thought it was funny. I mean, it took her five minutes of laughing before I could get her to sign for it. She told me that the guy who sent it to her was pissed off because she wasn't going to drop her son off at the sitter for a month and go with him to Vegas to go gambling. She said he needed to get his head on straight. After that, I never went on deliveries, nor did I talk to the people who gave the orders to me. It was just too much when they thought they had to explain why they were doing this. My way was much easier back then."

"And now? What will you do now? You're kinda out here, aren't you?" Yes, she supposed she was, but only shrugged. "I think you're going to do very well. You'll have to. I'm not working now."

Phillip started to help her, but she sent him on his way. He had things to do as well. And after giving him a list of people that she'd worked with that had dealt in antiques as well as objects that weren't easily found, she set to work on the desk again. Things were beginning to look up.

~~~

Max moved to the door of his new building and thought of the person who was coming to open the store for him. It would be an antique store for not just furniture, but for all sorts of things. Books and tables, of course, but he wanted to fill it with things like comic books and old phones that worked. Clothing that was so out of date it would be wonderful. He could see the displays that he'd have to help set up, as well as the old fashioned cash register that he already had his eye on online. Things were going to come together as soon as the woman came to town.

He had no idea who she was. Or what she was, for that matter. But he'd dreamt of her. Her long hair, her blue eyes. She'd be perfect for the store that he had in mind, and for so much more. She was for his uncle. And when they came together, neither of them would be the same again.

"Which one?" He looked over at his mom, completely forgetting that she'd come with him. "Andrew or Rider? Which uncle is going to murder you in your sleep for doing this to them until they figure out that you were right all along?"

"I don't know." She nodded at him as if she didn't believe him, but Max really didn't know. "She's beautiful, but not alone. I'm not sure what that means, but she has something with her that she protects."

"A child?" Max told her that he didn't think so. It just didn't feel like a child. "Well, it doesn't matter, I guess. Either one of the other two will love and protect her."

"Yes, we all will."

His mom moved to the place he'd already said was going to be the office. There was a huge safe in the office that had not been opened since the other owners had left in a hurry. He knew that it was full of things, but not what they were. He thought the walls too thick for him to breach, but also thought that it might be more than that. When she was close enough to the safe and to him, Max reached out and hugged her to him. And when she hugged him back, he felt him.

"Can you open this?" He shook his head. He knew that it could be opened, but not how to do it. The combination was somewhere in his building, but it wasn't his to find just yet. "You're being very mysterious, you know that, right? Why is that, I wonder?"

"Perhaps it's because I want to have some of my own secrets. Like you do." His mom asked him what he was talking about. "The baby. When were you going to tell me? I'm not stupid, you know."

"No, you're not. But we were kinda waiting for your party to be over with first. We didn't want to take away from the fact that you've finished college at the top of your class." He nodded, embarrassed now. "Do you suppose you can live with having a little sister or brother around?"

"Brother, though I wouldn't mind either, and yes. I'd like that." He looked at her, wondering if she'd known it was a boy or not. "Did I mess up by telling you that?"

"No. I sort of knew. I haven't told Carter yet because he's been hoping for a girl. There's not been that many born to this family, in the event you missed that." Max told her that everyone would be happy no matter what they had.

Aunt Hannah was due in a month. She'd have a boy as well. And Linyah was going to have a girl. Her little girl was already starting to show herself as much like her mother. Stubborn and magical as well. He looked at his mom when he realized that he'd missed something. She asked him what he knew about the woman coming here.

"Nothing. She's been on her way for some time. Not to here but in this direction. I'm not calling her here but I think something is. The shop will be for her. My store, of course, but she'll run it. That's the job you're going to offer her when she comes to you."

"She's coming to me before her mate?" He told her that it was the way he'd seen it. "And whatever she's bringing with her...what do you know about that other than it's not a child?"

"It's not a child and she is very...I guess tired of it. Something about it...while she needs to protect it, she doesn't all that much care for whatever it is." Murph nodded, as if she understood. "Were you ever tired of me? I know that it was a lot of work to keep me safe. Did you ever want to just say screw it and leave me with the sitters?"

"Every day. And while I was at it, I thought it would be just as easy to cut out the other half of my beating heart too. You know, to leave behind with the rest of it." He grinned at her. "Don't be a goof. I could no more leave you behind than I could hate you. You were my world then and now. I love you."

"I love you too. And Dad. I know that he's not my real father, but I don't think I could have gotten a better one. Uncles and aunts, too. They're amazing. Especially when we all get together."

His mom's radio went off, and she picked it up. She was the sheriff in town, and he knew that she had to go out again.

"I have to run. Will you be able to get home from here?" He told her that he'd call Carter and have him come to get him. "Good. Don't wait up. Mr. Gross has an intruder again. I will be late."

Mr. Gross had an intruder weekly. There was never anyone at his house, but Mom went and looked into it every single time he called. He might be crying wolf now, but that didn't mean that someday the big bad wolf wouldn't show up for him. Max also knew that there were any number of people watching over him. He was never going to be caught unawares. He called Carter to let him know what was going on.

"All right. How about you and I go and gather up as many of your uncles as I can find and we have dinner together? Misha is in town with me helping to close down the shop, Thomas is on his way home from the castle, and I think that Rider is in town buying groceries. What do you think?" He told him he'd love that. "Good. And so you know, you're buying."

"But I'm just a kid." Carter laughed and told him he was never a kid. "But you know that I have to save my money. I have no job now that you guys have quit yours."

"Get real, kid. You have as much if not more than all of us. And probably more than my tight-fisted brother Rider has. But you have a point. I'll pay, but you pick up the tip." Max said he would. "Okay. Walk down to the offices and be careful. I'll see you in a few minutes."

Max closed his phone and started turning off the lights to his building. He felt the vibrations of the people that had been here before him. There were many who had come and worked here, when the building had been a sewing factory for children's shirts. Max smiled as he turned out the last light and went to the door.

She was there then, the woman from his dreams. Not really there, he supposed, but he could see in her in the glass of the front door. Her long hair was wet this time, her face covered in mud. She wasn't hurt, but she was tired. Max wanted to reach out to her and tell her it was going to be fine, but she faded away then. As he locked up behind him, all he could think about was how the woman was going to be happy here. And so was he. Max decided that he loved having a family, a big one, and could not wait until they were all mated. It was going to be a great family when they all came together for meals.

Before You Go...

HELP AN AUTHOR

write a review

THANK YOU!

Share your voice and help guide other readers to these wonderful books. Even if it's only a line or two your reviews help readers discover the author's books so they can continue creating stories that you'll love. Login to your favorite retailer and leave a review. Thank you.

AWARD WINNING, BESTSELLING AUTHOR

Kathi Barton, author of the bestselling series Force of Nature, lives in Nashport, Ohio with her husband Paul. In addition to writing full time Kathi likes to spend time with her eight grandkids, three children and three children-in-laws. She writes to relax and have fun.

Her muse, a cross between Jimmy Stewart and Hugh Jackman brings them to life for her readers in a way that has them coming back time and again for more. Her favorite genre is paranormal romance with a great deal of spice. You can visit Kathi on line and drop her an email if you'd like. She loves hearing from her fans. aaronskiss@gmail.com.

Follow Kathi on her blog:
http://kathisbartonauthor.blogspot.com/